The Art of Death:

Alex's Story

A Christian Rinaldi Novella
By Derek Dorr

Derek Dorr

ISBN 13: 978-0692267141
ISBN: 069226714X

Published: Derek Dorr, August 4, 2014
Editing: Heather Stocks Pixley
Cover Design: Clarise Tan
Formatting by: Brenda Wright
This book is intended for a mature audience of eighteen and older.

Derek Dorr

<u>Acknowledgements</u>

I would like to thank my family, friends and readers (both existing and future) for helping to make my dreams come true. This journey wouldn't be possible without the support and sacrifices made by my wife, Janene, and our 3 adorable children. They have been very understanding about the many late nights that I have spent in my office.

I would also like to thank: my editor, Heather Stocks Pixley for cleaning up my frequent punctuation issues. Brenda Wright for all of your help with formatting, proofreading and going above and beyond on several other creative projects. Emily Bak for being my beta and head cheerleader. Jackie Day for spending several late nights being my sounding board and head of Canadian promotions, this story is better because of your input. Melissa Prentiss for taking on the role of assistant and spending tireless hours doing the dirty work so I could write. My street team for spreading my name to as many people as possible, there are too many of you to name individually.

Thank you, everyone for all that you do. If I have forgotten anyone, I apologize. Please know that I am honored and humbled by the responses to my writing and I hope to continue to share my stories with you for the foreseeable future. You all make my life better simply by being in it.

Table of Contents

Age: Three Years

"I think you drove by it, George," Edith naggingly said as she leaned far enough across the front seat of their rented Buick that George could barely see the road ahead. The tops of palm trees lining the sidewalks were his only guide. Their big green leaves kept him from hitting anyone or anything on this quiet Miami street.

"Edie, will you please sit down and buckle up? I can't see a darned thing with you in my lap," George calmly replied. Over the last 30 years of being married to the same woman, he had learned to pick his battles. The funny thing was that the older he got, the fewer battles felt like they were worth the fight.

"I am just trying to find the number. That one says 3125 and we need 3160 Seaside Ave, right? Do you think we should get out and walk?" Edie asked.

"Nah, we will find it. She isn't even expecting us for another hour, so we have plenty of time," George said in an attempt to calm his blushing bride's nerves.

"There's her car!" Edie yelled.

For the first time since they left the airport rental station, George nearly lost control of the car. It wasn't so much the sudden scream that threw him off—he was used to the wild swings in her speaking volume—it was actually her left arm that did the trick. It shot up in perfect synchrony with her vocal outburst and struck him squarely under his chin, causing his head to tilt upward sharply.

Even with his eyes staring at the padded roof and his square framed glasses half off his face, George maintained control of both the 2 ton vehicle and his temper.

"I think you are right," George said as he looked for a place to turn around. He pulled the boat of a car into the next available driveway and backed into the street. The enormous vehicle stretched into the opposite lane, but he was able to get it back on the proper side before any other cars came through.

The Parkers slowed as they passed what looked like their niece's ten-year-old mud brown Chevelle. At least a dozen parking tickets of various colors flapped in the breeze, pinned to the glass by the driver's side windshield wiper. A muted yellow parking violation "boot" on the rear tire ensured that it wasn't going anywhere. The amount of black brake dust on the boot from passing cars gave the car the appearance of being abandoned.

"Well, that isn't a good sign," George said as he pulled the Buick to a stop in a parking spot four down from the Chevelle.

"If she needed money, why didn't she call or write? She was never shy about it before," Edie said as she stepped gingerly onto the curb. At 50 years old, she wasn't as spry as she used to be. The two flights and forty-minute car ride to get from Maine to Miami had her feeling stiff all over.

George put his light blue fedora on his head and looked for the round ended key that the young man from the rental agency said would lock the car. Edith stood on the sidewalk facing a 9-story apartment building and waited for him to join her. With her robin's egg blue ankle length sundress, large floppy hat, and oversized purse resting in the crook of her elbow, she could easily have been heading into a church for Sunday services rather than checking on her niece.

Karen, the only daughter of Edie's late older sister, had moved to Miami almost four years prior. At first, all appeared well—she had a great fiancé and a newborn baby girl named Alexandra. The Christmas cards painted the picture of a perfect little family. It seemed almost too good to be true, and that was because it was all an act.

Behind the smiling faces and matching sweaters was an abusive relationship, both verbally and physically. No one knew for sure, but the rumor was that Karen gave as good as she got. Finally, the family fractured and her calls became less frequent. No one had heard from her in over a month. Karen was an adult and she could make her own decisions, but there was a child involved. The Parkers felt obligated to check in on them, so Edie sent a letter a week ago stating her non-negotiable plans to visit, and after 7 days without a response, here they were.

Edie tightly gripped George's right arm as they ascended the three flights of dirty stairs to the floor where Karen's apartment should be. She did her best to walk in the center of the stairs and had decided that she was throwing out any part of her outfit (or George's) that came in contact with the grungy walls, not matter how brief.

"Here we are, apartment 303," George said after they traversed forty feet of equally disgusting hallway. The flickering of the few working fluorescent lights made identifying the right apartment more of a challenge, but nonetheless, they made it.

"Karen dear, it is Aunt Edith and Uncle George," Edie said in a singsong voice as she reluctantly knocked on the door to 303.

"Kiki, Hun. Remember, she goes by Kiki now," George reminded her.

"Oh, that's right. I forget. What kind of name is Kiki for a grown woman, anyway? It sounds like a name you would see on the nametag of a waitress in a truck stop," Edie said between knocks.

Minutes passed and George contemplated a trip back down the stairs to look for the super, even if only to get away from the sound of his wife's voice reverberating off of the walls of the empty hallway. He grabbed the doorknob to give it a rattle but instead of the expected resistance of a locked door, he felt it turn the full way. The door had been unlocked the whole time.

"Kiki, it's Uncle George. Call out if you aren't decent. Otherwise, we are coming in," he said as he stuck his head through the open door. A musty smell similar to week-old wet cardboard filled his nostrils, causing him to gag slightly.

"Karen, are you in here?" Edie asked as she pushed the door fully open and walked past her still-leaning husband. She had also decided that she didn't like the way that nickname felt leaving her mouth so she would be using Karen's proper name from here on out.

Crusty food-covered dishes overfilled the small kitchen sink. Most of the cupboards were stained rusty orange over the top of an off-white paint, likely from nicotine as the air felt heavy with years of cigarette smoke. Spots of various colors from indistinguishable sources covered the green and gold shag carpet on all of the floors. It flowed from room to room without any visible difference from one space to the next. Well-worn lines in the carpet guided them along their journey like game trails in a meadow.

Edie opened the first available window and waved her hat toward the fresh air, fighting a losing battle to move the stale stuff out. The apartment barely had any furniture, aside from a flattened futon and milk crates for coffee tables. It seemed devoid of all life until they reached the final room.

In the second of two bedrooms, George found Alexandra. Instead of sitting on the stained, uncovered mattress that was thrown haphazardly into the corner next to a pile of possibly-clean toddler clothes, she was sitting on the floor with her feet behind her, forming either an M or W with her legs, depending on your angle of view.

She was stark naked aside from her diaper, which was so full that it was spilling out from around the legs and the top, and several layers of grime. Feces had crept up her back, and based on the different amounts of dryness, ranging from crusty and cracking to pasty, she must have been wearing this single diaper for the past several bowel movements.

An empty box of sugary cereal lying on the floor next to her was the only indication that she had eaten recently. Other than the bits of food on her cheeks, that is. Her ribs were visible and she lacked the normal body fat of a toddler. Even her cheekbones protruded under her sleep-deprived eyes.

Edie took a couple of quick steps toward the tiny girl, who promptly scurried away. George tried a less-aggressive approach and sat on the floor near where she had been. He picked up the nubs of crayons that she had been using to scribble on a second cereal box; this one was ripped open to expose the untouched cardboard inside. After a minute or so, she crawled over to him and watched as he added to her drawings.

Fifteen minutes of silent tandem-coloring won Alexandra over enough to allow George to pick her up. He gently replaced her soiled diaper with a clean one that Edie had scrounged up from another room. George's eyes welled with tears of angry sadness when he pointed to a multitude of scabbed-over round scars on her back. Even to a non-smoker, it was obvious that these were burns inflicted by the tip of a red-hot cigarette.

Edie looked away as George finished dressing the little girl. He had never had any children of his own, but as he looked into Alexandra's bright green eyes, he asked himself how anyone could hurt someone so small and defenseless. He didn't know the answer, but he did know that no one would ever do it again as long as he was around.

Edie dug through her purse, pulling out anything that a 3-year-old could possibly eat, and handed Alexandra a package of crackers and peanut butter. Alexandra's teeth were nothing more than bystanders as she shoved one salty treat after another into her mouth. When those four were gone, she reached out for more. Edie's heart broke when she had to shake her head to say that there weren't any more to give.

Six hours and two delivered meals later, the sun had just started to descend toward the ocean, when a noise startled the Parkers. Someone crashed into the outside of the apartment door before struggling to get it open. It swung open and slammed into the wall with enough force to crack the drywall, if it hadn't already been cracked.

Karen "Kiki" Miller stumbled through the open doorway with her arms draped around a Cuban man with a shaved head and several neck tattoos. He would later be recalled as "Rico". She was completely oblivious to the visitors until Rico noticed Edie standing with her arms crossed in front of her. Without a word, Rico turned and ran through the door he had just walked through seconds earlier.

Rico may have escaped the wrath of Hurricane Edith, but Kiki was not so lucky. Hours of festering rage boiled over when Edie's eyes met Kiki's glossy stare. She reached forward with the speed of a striking rattler and snatched her niece by the back of her head. A handful of greasy, stringy hair became a handle that Edie used to drag Kiki unwillingly through the apartment and into the bathroom.

For a woman of advanced middle age, Edie was quite strong. She nearly pulled Kiki off of her feet as she swung her toward the open tub. Kiki landed hard on the back side of the bathtub with her feet sticking out over the rim. Edie turned on the cold water and moved the lever from tub to shower setting and watched as drop after drop of freezing cold water cascaded down onto her either drugged-out or drunken family member.

George carried Alexandra into the hall to keep her from witnessing the fury that Edie was about to unleash. It didn't work. Even at the far end of the hallway, Edie's shouts could be heard. Apparently the other residents were used to screaming and yelling, as no one even opened their doors.

Twenty minutes or so passed before Edie's sermon about Karen's selfishness ended. When it finally concluded, George and Alexandra rejoined the two women. Karen sat on the futon, soaking wet and wrapped in a towel over her clothing, looking like the proverbial drowned rat.

"You have 5 minutes to change into something presentable and pack yourself some clean clothes. You and that baby are coming home with us," Edie ordered.

Kiki started to protest but thought better of it. She disappeared into the room next to Alexandra's and almost exactly five minutes later, she reappeared with two stuffed bags.

George and Edith Parker did a noble thing that day when they took in a young Alexandra Miller, but one has to wonder if they would have done the same thing or called Child Protective Services instead if they knew that the cute little red haired girl would grow up to become a ruthless killer. Maybe they would have found similar nobility in her mission to rid the world of men like the one who gave her those first scars, or maybe, just maybe, they would have made that call to CPS and waited across the street until someone came before walking away forever.

<u>Age: Six Years</u>

April 15th started like it had most any year in George's memory. He sat at the kitchen island with his newspaper, coffee, and buttered toast, and peered over the top of headlines about "Tax Day" at the birds munching away at his half dozen wooden bird houses spread across his back lawn. Edie was putting a load of whites in to wash while complaining about an errant piece of colored clothing that had somehow managed to sneak its way into the basket. It arrived there by nefarious means, no doubt about it.

Alex, as she now liked to be called most of the time (Lexi was also acceptable), was in her usual spot as well, sitting cross-legged on the braided rug in front of the small television in the den. She had gotten in the habit of watching the weather on the local news before picking out her school clothes for the day. Her mother snored away one floor above her, exhausted from her evening shift as a CNA in a local nursing home, and in all likelihood, hung over for good measure.

Most weekdays started in a similar manner, but this one was going to be different and it all started with a car pulling into the driveway and a knock on the door.

George didn't see the car and was surprised by the knock. The sight of two uniformed Bentonville Police Department Officers only added to the shock.

"Good morning Ben," George said to the first officer who he had known since the young man was born. "How can I help you?"

"I am sorry to bother you, Mr. Parker, but we got a call and you know we have to follow up on everything. It is probably just a crank call, but you know how it is," Ben stammered, rubbing the back of his head. The usually confident police officer was evidently uncomfortable about the whole situation.

"Sure, come on in," George said, holding the door open so that Officer Ben and his partner could enter the kitchen. "What did the call say?"

"Well," Ben started before his partner interrupted him.

"The caller said that someone was dealing drugs out of this house," said the second officer who George didn't recognize.

"Like I said, probably just a crank," Ben said. "Do you mind if we take a look around so we can go back to the station and sign off?"

Before George could answer, Edie walked into the kitchen. She had been listening in from the laundry room and was not in the mood for an intrusion. "Ben Bailey, you can't be serious. What do you think we are selling? Blood pressure medicine?"

"I didn't say I believed it, Mrs. Parker. I just have to follow up," Officer Bailey said sheepishly.

"Well, you caught me. I have been dealing to the women's rotary and my Sunday canasta group. I have been trying to get into the Tuesday Bingo night crowd over at the VFW, but Esther Timmons beat me to it. Might as well cuff me now before I try and run," Edie said sarcastically, sticking her hands out in front of her and crossing them at the wrists.

"Now Edie, cut that out. Let the young man do his job for crying out loud," George said curtly before turning to the two officers still standing in his kitchen entry. "Let me go get Alex so you don't startle her and then you can do whatever you need to."

Officer Bailey nodded in agreement, but his partner stepped forward and put a hand out to block George from leaving the room. "I am sorry sir, but I can't permit you to go anywhere without an escort until we have fully searched the premises.

Again, before George could mount a protest of his own, Edie stepped in. "You are not going to scare that little girl before she heads off to kindergarten for the day. I am going to go into my den and bring her out here. If I even see you poke your head around the corner, you will need to arrest me for assaulting a police officer. Your choice."

No one moved other than Edie who disappeared into the back of the house. Neither Officer Bailey or George spoke, but both had to look away to conceal the smirks spreading across their faces. Officer Joe Rohn, Bailey's partner of three weeks, stood in silence, fuming as his face turned a couple shades of pink.

"George, is there anyone else in the house that we should know about?" Bailey asked when he could finally stop smiling.

"Yes, my niece, Karen, is sleeping upstairs. Do you want me to go get her?" George asked.

"No, Officer Rohn is right, we can't let you go up there alone," Bailey responded.

"How about I just yell up from the bottom of the stairs? That is how we usually wake her up anyway," George suggested.

Bailey and Rohn exchanged looks and Bailey said, "I don't see why not. Just don't tell her that we are here."

George walked through the living room and stopped at the bottom of the stairs. "Karen, can you come down here and say goodbye to Alex?"

"Give me 5 minutes," Karen yelled back, the sleepiness evident in her voice.

A muffled thump emanating from the space directly above the living room was followed by an uncoordinated series of footsteps through the upstairs, and then down the staircase as a door slammed shut behind Karen. She was still rubbing her eyes as she appeared in the living room clad in a white tee shirt that hung loosely off of her right shoulder and a pair of plaid men's boxer shorts. The brief but intense period of her life filled with alcohol, drugs, and overall hard living was supposed to be in the past, but it had taken its toll. Before it was done with her, that lifestyle had aged her appearance well beyond what her actual 25 years should have.

"What the hell?" she asked when she saw the two uniformed men standing only half a room away.

"Ma'am, could you join us in the kitchen please?" Officer Bailey asked, standing a tad taller and straighter than he had been.

"Jesus Christ Ben, what is with the 'ma'am' shit? I've barely got 3 years on you," Karen snapped.

Edie and Alex stepped into view at the other end of the house. Edie stood protectively behind Alex with both hands on the small girl's shoulders. Alex was now fully dressed for school in a pair of jeans and a Smurfette tee shirt. A pair of pigtails added to the picture of adorableness. She hated the way her hair felt on her ears and neck, so pigtails would become a staple hair style option throughout her life. A Barbie backpack sat on the floor near the kitchen door with one strap stretched out slightly more than the other due to her preference of only having it slung over one shoulder.

"Can I take her out to wait for the bus or do you need to pat her down first?" Edie asked, the irritated sarcasm still bitingly evident in her tone.

"You can let her go out to wait but I need you to stay inside, Ma'am," Rohn responded. It was clear that he was not amused by Edie and he wasn't about to give her any leeway. This investigation was going to be by the book. If she was going to push buttons, he intended to push right on back. Unfortunately for him, he was picking a fight that he had zero chance of winning.

"If you think for one second that I am going to let her stand out by the edge of the road by herself, you are even dumber than those big ears and goofy face make you look. I will be back in when she is sitting on the bus and not a second before," Edie said. Her eyes narrowed into thin angry slits and the room almost felt colder.

"You'll be able to see them through that picture window," George said to Rohn, pointing to the large window in the living room. He was trying to save the poor boy from getting himself hurt, and he really hoped that Rohn backed down. "Just pull the curtain back some and you can see the spot where they stand."

Rohn didn't speak or even nod. Doing so would have been admitting defeat, and his stubborn young ego was getting in the way of reasonable decisions.

"Will someone please tell me what is going on?" Karen asked again from her new seat on the couch.

The men turned to look at her in unison and Edie took the chance to walk Alex out. Before Edie and Alex were able to get outside, the large, yellow school bus sped by without even so much as a honk or wave. Edie took a chance that the snotty little brat wearing a badge in her living room didn't notice the passing bus. She simply led Alex to the end of the driveway as usual.

"We missed the bus, Aunt Edie. Are you going to drive me to school?" Alex asked, her large emerald green eyes full of confusion.

"Yes Hun, I will take you as soon as those men leave," Edie replied with a pat on the head.

"Why are they here? Did Mommy do something wrong again?" Alex asked.

"No one said anything about your mom. Why would you think that?" Edie questioned.

"The police put bad people in jail and you and Uncle George are too old to be bad," Alex answered. Her response was one of a clear-cut honesty that only children have. By the time most people are teenagers, their internal filter won't allow such unrestrained yet simple thinking to occur.

Back inside the normally quiet house, Rohn was busy lifting couch cushions and digging through cupboards while Bailey watched George and Karen. Bailey was already satisfied and wanted to leave, but something about the way that Karen was acting had him suspicious.

Karen was still sitting on the couch, but now she was leaning forward with her hands together between her tightly pressed knees. Her legs bounced up and down, displaying a kind of fidgety nervousness that Bailey commonly saw in junkies who had been sitting in a holding cell overnight. She kept looking back toward the stairs.

"Is everything okay, Karen?" Bailey asked.

His voice seemed to startle her and she jumped slightly. "Everything is fine. I just need to use the bathroom. Is it cool if I run up and use it?"

"Sorry, but he hasn't cleared that part of the house yet. He has done the one down here, so you could use that if you wanted to," Bailey answered.

"I'll wait. I like my bathroom better. More privacy. Are you sure I can't just run up real quick?"

Bailey just shook his head. Rohn had just finished the downstairs and started walking up the stairs when Karen grew more agitated.

"Hey, you can't go in my room or touch my stuff. I got personal stuff that I don't want touched, you know. It is an invasion of my privacy," she insisted.

"Karen, our warrant is for the entire property and any structures on it. He won't break anything, I promise," Bailey reassured her. It didn't help.

Karen opened her mouth to speak but the stomping of Rohn's boots on the stairs stopped her. Rohn turned the corner, unable to hide his smile.

"Probably a crank call? That is what you said, isn't it Officer Bailey?" the smug young man asked.

"Yes."

"Then what is this?" Rohn asked as he pulled a gallon-sized freezer bag from behind his back. The bag was three quarters full of much smaller baggies containing a white powder. "It could be powdered sugar, but I am thinking more like, oh I don't know, cocaine. Feels like a pound or so."

"Karen, please tell me that isn't what he says," George pleaded. Karen didn't respond. She simply looked away.

"I would say that between the hundreds of packages in here, the empty baggies, and cash that I found in the room at the top of the stairs, someone here is going away on felony drug possession and intent to distribute. Wouldn't you agree, Bailey?" Rohn asked.

"If that is drugs, then yes," Bailey answered quietly.

"Now the only question I have is who goes to jail today. Is it him, the mouthy broad outside, the junkie-looking chick, or all three? I can't decide. It was her room, but they own the house. Maybe we should just load everyone up and call social services to pick up the kid until we sort this all out," Rohn said, relishing every unnecessarily drawn out moment.

"Joe, don't be a di...," Bailey began to say. Rohn's eyebrows rose as he waited for the end of the sentence.

"It was mine," Karen said softly.

"I am sorry, what did you say?" Rohn asked, leaning closer to the seated woman.

"I said they were mine, you asshole," Karen said.

"Cuff her while I bag the evidence," Rohn said to a reluctant Bailey.

The sight of her mother being driven away, cuffed in the back of a blue and white police car, would be the first of the final dozen times that Alex would see her mother. The next would be two weeks later when a judge, who reminded Alex of an angry beardless Santa Claus, sentenced Karen to 25 years in prison, of which she would serve just under two years. Alex would see her at the prison for holidays, her mother's birthday, and two of her own birthdays. In fact, the final two times that she would see her mother would turn out to be on Alex's 8th birthday and then again when she was 8 years and 5 days old. Those final two visits would stay in her memories and frequent her dreams for the rest of Alex's life.

Alex's 8th Birthday

Alex watched the rain fall through the window in the back seat of Uncle George's Impala. She knew she was supposed to be happy today, but she couldn't manage the same enthusiasm as the rest of the people around her. The full truth was that she rarely, if ever, felt the way other people seemed to about the events of their lives. She didn't feel sad or happy or excited or any of the other words that people used to describe themselves. She wasn't truly sure that she understood what they meant. People might as well have been saying that they "felt spaghetti today", it would mean as much.

Many of the people around Alex would say things like, "You would be so pretty if you just smiled more." or tried to get her to laugh by tickling her. Some talked to her directly about her lack of a mood, but many just talked to those around her as though she wasn't there. The common response was "Well, she has had a rough life."

Alex, on the other hand, didn't see her life as particularly difficult. She lived with her mother's aunt and uncle instead of with her parents like other kids, but that didn't bother her. She had been to lots of kids' homes who had parents that treated them worse than George and Edie treated her. She loved them both very much and they loved her back. Who cared that they weren't her real parents?

Aunt Edie had fallen into the motherly role after Karen (she refused to call her "Mom") had gone to jail. She did everything a mother should do, and she did it well. Sometimes she was a bit overprotective, but that was fine too. There were times where she made Alex feel like Edie thought she was fragile, but that wasn't often. Alex just hoped that someday she would stop saying, "I know I am not your mother but..."

George, on the other hand, didn't try to be the fill-in father type. He loved to spend time with her, and some of her happiest moments were spent with him in his shop, learning how he made his famous birdfeeders. She is always amazed to watch a piece of wood and a bucket of paint turn into a work of art. George asks her questions about her day and is a great listener when she opens up, but unlike everyone else, he doesn't try to jump in and tell her how to fix it. That is probably why she likes to talk with him more than she does other people.

"Are you nervous, hun? You are so quiet," Edie asked from the front seat, nearly turning completely around to face her.

"Not really," Alex answered.

"I am sure your mother will be excited to see you. I can't believe how much you have grown since she last saw you," Edie continued.

That was true. Alex had grown about 4 inches in the last few months and was now taller than most of the other kids in her class—even the boys. Things like that didn't matter to her, either. The only part about growing that much that did upset her was that it meant that George and Edie had to buy her more clothes. George worked at a newspaper printing company four nights a week and was ready to retire soon. Edie worked part-time at a local arts and crafts store, but couldn't work too many hours and still be around for Alex. They never said anything to her, but Alex knew that money was tight. They had never planned on raising a child this late in life.

The car took a left turn onto a quieter road and Alex recognized the turn as the last one before they would reach the Maine Women's Correctional Facility. In just a few minutes, they would drive through the huge metal gate with the razor wire on top. They would all have to sign a piece of paper saying why they were there, and then a guard would pat each of them down, looking for stuff that they couldn't take in with them. After that, they would walk into large open room and sit on one side of the table while they waited for Karen. She could hug each of them, but not for long, and then they got a half hour to talk.

Karen would ask Alex a bunch of questions like she always did and Alex would answer them, even though she didn't want to. What she wanted to say was "Why do you care?" or one of the many other things that she had practiced in her head. Alex's therapist said that she should "vocalize her feelings" more and that would make her feel better. Maybe this would be the visit.

*   *   *   *   *

Karen sat on the edge of her bunk and watched as the second hand ticked around the face of the wall clock. She occasionally lost sight of it behind one of the thin metal bars that protected it from being broken or ripped down.

Today was going to be a special day. She had an unwrapped present sitting on her lap, a certificate of completion from her drug rehab program saying that she was finally one year sober. She also had letters that she wanted to give to Alex. She had written them with the help of her counselor as a way of explaining her actions and saying how sorry she was.

All of Karen's hard work was paying off for her. She was clean and sober, she had a good job in the prison's library, and she was even trying to earn a degree so that she could be a counselor when she got out. She wanted to help people like her to solve their problems before they ended up in a cold, windowless six-foot by eight-foot concrete cell like the one she sat in now.

These changes had come at a price, though. To kick her habit, she had broken ties with her prison dealer, Tiny. Tiny had not taken it lightly. She had protected Karen when she first arrived and needed help. She had given Karen a job as a dealer in her cell-block, and then Karen just turned her back on her.

Tiny had confronted Karen in the lunch room and got so angry that she had to be restrained by the guards.

Thankfully, they were in different cell-blocks now, but the threat was always there. Tiny had a lot more friends in here than Karen did.

Finally, a loud buzz told Karen that it was time to go. The door to her cell rattled open and she stepped out into the openness of the general population floor. Not all of the doors had opened, just the ones for people with visitors. Karen always worried on visitation days that she would hear the buzz but her door would stay shut. She told herself that she would be prepared for that moment if it came, but she knew better. Her heart would break if Alex stopped coming.

Karen took a quick look around at the other women who would be joining her in the visitation room. Almost everyone was openly excited. Some were obviously nervous, but the air was electrified by their emotions. The only one who seemed out of place was Dee, one of the women who used to protect Karen. She stared straight ahead, focused on something that Karen couldn't see.

Karen's heart pounded as she stepped into the single-file line that would lead her to her baby girl. Her palms were sweaty and she wiped them down the sides of her brown prison-issue jumpsuit. She was so nervous that she almost crinkled up the papers in her hand. Only a few minutes more.

She walked slowly, but in unison with the others as they all moved closer and closer to visitation. As always, someone in the back stepped too close to another person and they all pushed forward. Surprisingly, this didn't result in shouting or pushing and shoving as it would have in the chow line.

As each person reached the entrance door, they had to give the final guard their name. The guard checked the clipboard to confirm that their loved one was indeed in the room, and then they could proceed.

Only one person was ahead of Karen now, and that was Dee. Dee spoke to the guard who then looked at the clipboard and waved her in. Dee walked to the middle of the room, looked around and nodded at a man sitting at a table on the left side, but she didn't move. Karen didn't think a lot about it as she stepped up to the guard.

"Name?" the guard asked in the usual perfunctory manner.

"Karen Miller," Karen answered.

"You have three visitors. Remember, you may give them each a short hug hello and goodbye. No other touching is allowed. You may only accept an item from them that has been screened and approved. Do you understand?" the guard recited from memory.

"Yes," Karen answered.

"Have a good visit, inmate," the guard said, stepping aside so Karen could walk into the room. They always called them "inmate" like they needed to remind them that they were not really people anymore. They were all something less than that.

Karen walked into the visitation room and searched the mass of people for the small round table where her family was sitting. Each table was bolted to the floor as were all the chairs. The room itself looked like a 40-year-old cafeteria, complete with horrendous fluorescent lighting.

She spotted George, Edie, and Alex sitting in the middle of the room. Excitement washed over her and she wanted to run to them. Edie had on her best fake smile. She was obviously uncomfortable in this room, and even a half-dozen visits still hadn't made her feel less so. George's smile was genuine and welcoming. He always had a huge heart and Karen was glad that Alex had them both in her life.

She brushed past Dee who was still standing in the center of the room for some unknown reason. When she did, Dee started moving too. Strange.

"Oh my God, you have grown so much!" Karen squealed as she stepped within five feet of her table. That was when she felt it. Something slammed into her from behind and she felt a searing pain in her back in one spot, and then two, and then too many to count.

People screamed around her including Edie. George ran forward to catch her but was pushed away by the guards. Her certificate fell to the floor in front of her and a puddle of blood spread toward it. Whose blood was that?

* * * * *

Alex watched as Karen walked toward her. She was smiling and talked to her while waving a piece of paper. Alex couldn't hear what she was saying. Suddenly, a woman who had been standing in the middle of the room ran up behind Karen and grabbed her by the shoulder. She looked like she was punching Karen in the back because Karen was bulging forward a little each time.

Karen's eyes had a startled and scared feel to them. It wasn't something that Alex had seen before. Aunt Edie screamed for help and Uncle George ran around the table to catch Karen. Some guards grabbed the lady who had grabbed Karen and threw her to the ground. Others pushed Uncle George out of their way and picked up Karen. They dragged them both out of the room, but then took them in opposite directions.

Alex looked on the floor and saw several pieces of paper lying there. They were covered in Karen's blood. She knelt down to look at it closer. She didn't try to read the papers but saw her name and her mother's name on different ones, and recognized her mother's handwriting on some sheets of notebook paper. She reached down and touched the blood. It was warm and sticky and smelled like copper from Uncle George's shop.

Alex couldn't have cared less about the paper but she was mesmerized by the blood. This had been inside her mother just a few minutes ago, being moved around her body by the pumping of her heart, and now it was here, on the cold tile floor, doing nothing.

Only it wasn't doing *nothing*, it was most definitely doing something. The spilled blood sent a sensation through Alex. She loved the way it felt on her fingers. She wanted to splash in it the way other kids splashed in puddles. Her whole body tingled. She felt like she had never felt before and she loved it. Sitting there, running her fingers through a puddle of her own mother's freshly-spilled warm coagulating blood, Alex did something she had pretended to do many times before.

Alex smiled.

Five Days Later

"Alex, are you dressed yet?" Edie yelled from the bottom of the stairs.

Alex didn't answer right away. She had heard the question, but she was busy. She was not dressed. Her new black dress was still spread across the end of her bed. Aunt Edie had made her bed just before she laid the dress out, and put a pair of black tights next to it along with her black shoes.

Alex didn't want to get dressed. She had no interest whatsoever in going to Karen's funeral, let alone wearing a special dress for it. She would much rather continue to sit on her bedroom floor and play tug of war with her new puppy. Upon hearing about her mother's violent demise, one of her other uncles had decided that she should have a replacement. Three days ago, Alex had returned home from school and found a two-month-old golden retriever puppy waiting for her. She already loved it more than she could ever remember loving Karen.

The click-clack of Aunt Edie's dressy shoes on the stairs didn't even get her to start getting ready. The door opened and her aunt just stared at her for a second or two before speaking.

"Alex, I know this is a sad day but we really need to get going. You can't keep Spunky in here with you if he is going to distract you," Edie said before walking over to pick the small blonde dog up. His tiny legs kicked at the open air, trying to find something to climb on. He immediately started to lick her face when Edie held him against her.

"Now, please get dressed and come down when you are done," she said before closing the door behind her.

Alex heard the click-clack of the shoes on the stairs, and then on the hardwood floors in the living room, and finally on the tile of the kitchen. Spunky, named because George had said that the puppy had a lot of spunk, began whimpering in the distance. He only did that when he was in his kennel, so that must be where he ended up. Alex quickly dressed and ran down the stairs to meet her waiting family.

A half-hour later, Alex sat in the front row of chairs at the funeral home. She was in a big, plush, red-and-white chair while everyone else sat in folding chairs. The special chair must have been to remind everyone that it was *her* mother who was in the coffin.

Alex had looked in at her mother, lying there in the big wooden coffin—her head on a lace pillow, she was dressed in a beautiful sundress rather than her prison outfit and surrounded by flowers. Someone had applied makeup because she hadn't had any at the jail. Alex had touched her hand and face, which caused a few women to cry. They murmured about how she must be missing her mother and wanted to touch her one last time. That wasn't the case at all.

Alex felt almost nothing when she looked at her mother. She just wanted to know what it felt like to touch a dead person. Cold and stiff, was the answer. She turned and walked back to her chair and almost instantly, people swarmed around her.

"I am so sorry," one woman said, as many did.

"You are so brave," another commented.

Why am I brave? Alex wondered. She didn't do anything other than get dressed and come here with her Aunt and Uncle. What was brave about that?

Finally, a minister began to speak and everyone returned to their seats. The man in a black outfit with a white spot on his neck talked about how Karen had lived a tough life, made mistakes, and in the end had turned her life around. He talked about how she loved everyone, especially "young Alexandra", and how much Karen was loved by everyone.

He asked if people wanted to speak, and a few came to the podium and told stories about Karen when she was younger—her hopes and dreams. Many people behind Alex were crying. One woman in particular cried very loudly whenever Karen's name was said. They all spoke of a life cut short as though she had died in a car accident rather than getting shanked in prison by a woman who worked for her former drug dealer.

At the end of the ceremony, the minister asked Alex if she wanted to speak. She could talk about her mother as only a daughter could. She could share a happy story of her childhood or something like that. Alex said that she didn't want to speak and he ended the ceremony by saying that people could go to the cemetery to see her buried or they could go to George and Edie's for "refreshments and the sharing of memories" and that everyone should "celebrate your life and those in it before they are gone".

On the way home, Alex tried to think of what she could possibly have said. Karen was sent to prison when she was only in kindergarten. They hadn't lived on their own since she was 3, and she only had a few memories that she could remember well enough to share. She could talk about all the nights that she was locked in her room while Karen had men come to their apartment to pay her to be alone with them. She could talk about the time that a man took Alex to his apartment for three days until Karen paid him the money she owed. Or she could share the story about when one man said that he wanted to "play with Alex" and Karen freaked out and tried to kick him out of their apartment but got beaten instead. Which of those heartwarming stories would have been best?

Her quiet home was overrun by people for the rest of the day. Almost everyone tried to talk to her, but she just wanted to be alone. After an hour of constant questions, Alex managed to sneak out the door and around the garage. To her surprise, she wasn't the only one who had thought of hiding there.

"How are you holding up?" Uncle George asked, patting the bench next to him.

Alex didn't respond. She simply shrugged her shoulders.

"That good, huh?" George said as she sat down. "It will all be over soon. We won't see most of these people again until the next funeral. I am sorry that so many of them aren't leaving you alone."

"I miss the quiet," Alex admitted. "They all want to know if I am sad or to tell me that Karen was a great person."

"I know you aren't happy with her right now, kid. At some point in the future, you will miss her. You can come talk to me about it then," George said.

"Can I just sit here until they leave?" Alex asked.

"I can't say that but you can wait here until Aunt Edie starts looking," George responded.

Thankfully, Alex was asleep when Edie did find her. She was lying down with her head on George's lap. He stroked her hair as she slept and when Edie found them, he just picked Alex up and carried her to her room. She wasn't his daughter by birth, but she was as close as he was going to have and he loved every minute of it. Oh, and as for Alex eventually missing her mother, that still hasn't happened yet.

Age 11

"Shut up, Spunky!" Alex screamed across her back yard.

"He just wants to come play with us," said Toni, Alex's best, and possibly only, friend. The friendship had started as a forced pairing in second grade when they were the only children who didn't have a partner for a reading assignment. It had since grown into a genuine liking of each other. When the other kids fought over who they were going to partner with on future assignments, they always knew.

Alex and Toni have spent almost every weekend together over the past three years, aside from the occasional holiday, family vacation, and one ill-fated attempt by Toni's parents to send her to church camp the previous summer. Toni had turned from a friend of necessity to one of only four living creatures that Alex even remotely cared about. The other three were Aunt Edie, Uncle George, and Spunky, although that was not necessarily the order of affection.

"I know he does but he can't come over here and Aunt Edie doesn't want us playing over by him when it is muddy," Alex responded.

"Yeah I know, she doesn't want him ripping up her precious fucking flowerbeds," Toni said. She had recently started working a version of the "f-word" into as many conversations as she could, but only when adults were out of earshot.

"She said as soon as he stops being so destructive and hyper that we can let him run around. She calls it his 'puppy stage'," Alex said, ignoring the swearing.

Spunky was now three years old and still didn't show any signs of getting out of that "puppy stage". He loved to run, jump, and chew on anything he could. He had turned into a prolific digger and if given a chance, would remove every plant, bush, or bulb in Edie's gardens. The biggest issues were that he didn't seem to realize how big he had gotten or how dangerous other animals or even the nearby road could be. He was almost 75 pounds of energetic muscle and unintentionally knocked everyone who came within range to the ground.

Poor Spunky would be relegated to his dog house and the space that he could run around on via the strong steel cables that ran from one large pine to another and hooked to his collar, until he learned to follow Edie's rules. He no longer came in the house, let alone slept on Alex's bed like he used to. That didn't stop her from sneaking out and cuddling with him, though.

"Time for lunch!" Edie yelled to the girls through the sliding glass doors in the back of the house.

Alex and Toni began an impromptu race from the edge of the back yard to the back deck, serenaded by a chorus of barks and howls from Spunky. As usual, Toni reached the finish line a full step or so ahead of Alex. Neither girl slowed down as they bounded up the wooden steps and onto the large deck, the combination of their momentum and severe lack of coordination nearly causing them to crash through the screen of the open glass doors.

"You girls need to slow down or someone is going to get hurt," chided the ever-cautious Edie.

"Yes, Aunt Edie," both girls responded in practiced unison.

"Wash up and get yourselves a drink. There's iced tea and lemonade in the fridge," Edie instructed.

Both girls chose lemonade over the tea. Edie made her iced tea, as she did most things, by the old-fashioned route. She boiled water and soaked tea bags in it on her windowsill for most of a day before adding the ice cubes. It never had any sugar, and the girls found it to be bitter. The lemonade was made from fresh lemons and was quite sour in its own right, but Uncle George always managed to sneak sugar in when his wife wasn't looking.

The girls took up their usual seats on barstools around a high-topped kitchen island. The dining room table was only a few feet away, but that was only ever used for supper or family meals. Their bologna sandwiches and salt and vinegar chips were already waiting for them. Edie busied herself by cleaning her kitchen counters, wiping away a mess that was apparently only visible to her.

"Look at that fool dog out there standing on his house. I swear that thing is possessed," Edie said looking through the windows at the large golden retriever perched with his paws on each side of the pointed dog house roof.

"I think he is funny," Toni commented.

"Well one of these days, he is going to break his funny little neck," Edie said as she picked up her oversized purse from its usual spot on a table next to the kitchen's ancient telephone. She struggled to unwrap the long looping yellow phone cord from around her purse's shoulder straps. Finally freeing the mammoth purse, she turned to the seated preteens and said, "I have to run to the pharmacy. I am sure you don't want to go, do you?"

The girls shook their heads in response so Edie continued, "I shouldn't be more than 20 minutes or a half-hour tops, unless Gert is working, and then I will never get to leave. That woman is nothing but a gossip. No need for a newspaper with her around. Anyway, Uncle George is still sleeping from his overnight shift, so please be quiet. I expect you both to still be here when I get back. Understood?"

"Yes, Aunt Edie," the girls said in unison for the second time in as many minutes.

Alex and Toni spent the next thirty minutes playing in the back yard, jumping on the trampoline and doing anything else they could think of, but even two well-behaved children will test the limits of a household's rules when unsupervised for any length of time. Boredom had begun to set in as they sat on the trampoline, tired of jumping. They couldn't think of anything to do, but Spunky's barking gave Toni an idea.

"Why don't we let Spunky play with us?" she asked.

"Umm, because Aunt Edie would kill me. That's why," Alex responded sarcastically.

"Oh, come on, she won't be back for a while. He really wants to play, and besides, if she gets home before we put him back on, we can just say he got loose," Toni said with an all too familiar devious smirk.

Alex did want to play with her dog, but she didn't want to get in trouble either. Her hesitation was enough to cause her only human friend to mock her. "Oh, yeah, I forgot that you were a total goodie-goodie."

Alex's face burned with a flash of anger. Instead of responding to Toni directly, she stood and walked toward Spunky. As she got closer, the ever-happy dog began jumping straight into the air. He was such a strong jumper that his chest was reaching heights that were over either girl's head.

Alex held her hands in front of her body with her palms facing down, a command that Uncle George had used to train Spunky. The hyperactive mutt responded by crouching down, his entire body shaking from excitement. Alex reached down and after turning his collar a half rotation, unhooked the metal clasp of the run from the loop on the monogrammed collar. The collar was from L.L. Bean and had cost her over a month's allowance, but it was worth it.

At first, Spunky seemed to be confused by what was happening. He was only ever off his run if he needed to go to the vet or for his baths in the winter time. That changed as soon as Alex started to walk away. He ran circles around her, jumping into the air for attention.

With no sign of Aunt Edie returning, they became more brazen in their breaking of her rule. They started by tossing a ball for him to fetch, which devolved into a game of "chase Spunky" when he no longer wanted to give the ball up. They ran from one end of the field to the other until he ran in front of Alex while she was in midstride, causing them to crumble into a heap of boney knees and elbows, both human and dog.

Alex stood and wiped away a trickle of blood forming on a pale white scrape at the point of her elbow. Spunky licked the side of her face as his apology, but the sight of the blood was what Alex was interested in. In the years since her mother's violent death, spilled blood had become a source of fascination for her. It didn't matter who it belonged to or where it came from, the deep crimson liquid had a near hypnotic effect on Alex. On this particular afternoon, this blood trance led indirectly to the spilling of more innocent blood.

Alex continued to run the tip of her finger around her elbow before pulling it up to eye level to study it further. It spread over the tip of her index finger and down the sides and Alex was thinking that it looked like how hot fudge spreads over an ice cream sundae, when it happened. She didn't notice that Toni had thrown the tennis ball high into the air, nor did she see that it landed on the roof before rolling off the other side toward the front yard. She wasn't aware that Spunky bolted around the side of the house, nearly crashing into her along the way. No, it was the sound of screeching tires, loud thud and unrelenting yelps of pain that she first noticed in the furthest ends of her consciousness. Even then, it was Toni's screams that snapped her back to reality.

"OH MY GOD! SPUNKY!" Toni screamed.

Alex looked around and didn't see her friend or her loving furry companion. She wiped her blood onto her pants and ran to the front yard. What she saw hurt her heart in ways that not even watching her mother die had been able to do.

A man had pulled his car across their driveway and was yelling, "I couldn't even see him. He ran out in front of me as soon as I came around the corner."

Alex ignored the man who was pacing with his hands on top of his head, fingers interlaced, and walked toward Spunky. She stopped at the edge of the busy country road and watched as cars swerved around his mangled frame. He was nearly in the center of the road, his back legs twisted at an odd angle, unmoving. Spunky was whimpering in a high pitched and frantic tone as he used his front legs to drag his body closer to his favorite person and the safety of the grass.

Without looking in either direction, Alex stepped from the dirt and onto the asphalt road. She fearlessly took a half dozen more steps and squatted next to him. He stopped crawling and put his head on her bent knee and locked his eyes onto hers. They were still Spunky's eyes that she was peering into, but they looked different somehow. They were almost human in their ability to convey his message. He was in severe pain, confused about what happened, but most of all, his eyes begged for help. In that second, Alex knew why they seemed so odd to her. They looked exactly like her mother's did before she was carried away.

Horns honked and cars swerved around the crouching young girl and her dog, but Alex didn't pay attention to any of that. She was locked in on Spunky's eyes and occasionally the bones that jutted out of the fur on his legs. She could feel his heart pounding, like waves filling the space between them. She rubbed his head, hoping to calm him.

Out of nowhere, Alex felt her body being lifted and pulled away. She refused to let go of her dog and his damaged body dragged through the tar, gravel and eventually grass before they were both placed on the ground. In an instant, Uncle George's face was inches from her own, his hands on her shoulders shaking her. He was screaming at her, asking what happened, why she was in the road, and that she could have been killed. His voice was angry but his eyes showed the emotion behind the anger: fear.

Alex and Toni were taken into the house by the newly arrived Aunt Edie. She was so angry that she couldn't speak to either of them. That didn't stop Toni from trying to talk her way out of any blame. Alex watched as Uncle George carried Spunky into his shop at the rear of the garage. A minute later he came into the house and called a neighbor, Frances who was a retired vet of some type, Alex couldn't remember which. As soon as he hung up, Aunt Edie made Toni call her mother to pick her up.

Fifteen long, silent minutes later, Frances arrived and was taken to the makeshift animal clinic by Uncle George. Alex attempted to follow but was told that she needed to stay right where she was until her friend left. That took another five agonizing minutes.

Alex didn't even say "goodbye" to Toni when her mother arrived. As soon as her car pulled into the driveway, Alex ran for the shop where she found her uncle and the former vet talking. They were looking at Spunky who was spread across a low workbench. Uncle George had laid out several towels but Spunky was anything but comfortable. His whining was quieter and less frequent until Frances touched his back legs. George held him down as the former doctor's boney fingers poked and prodded Spunky's injured flesh.

"So, what do you think, Doc?" Uncle George asked with resigned hopefulness in his voice.

"It isn't good, George. He has broken both legs and it feels like his hip is crushed," the elderly woman responded.

"Should I take him to the animal hospital?" George said, less hopefully this time.

"If he just had one broken leg or even if both had clean breaks, I might say yes. His are broken in multiple places. They can't be saved, and sure, he could get by if he lost one, but that isn't an option. I don't even think there is enough bone left to put in rods, and even if there was, his hips are destroyed," Frances said solemnly, placing a hand on George's shoulder in an attempt to comfort an old friend. "I don't have anything to put him down at my house but I could call the hospital and have one of them come out here if you want."

"No, I'll handle it," Uncle George said, his eyes filling with tears.

"I do have some sedatives back at the house, I'm pretty sure. Let me go get some so he won't be hurting," Frances said.

"That would be nice of you. It will give Edie and Alex a chance to say their goodbyes. I don't know what I am going to tell that little girl," George said, wiping a tear from his cheek.

Her uncle still hadn't noticed Alex standing in the shadows so she slipped back into the main part of the garage and hid behind the car as Frances left. From her hiding place she could hear him sobbing as he softly spoke to Spunky about how sorry he was, that he was going somewhere nice, a place where he could run free, and that he loved him. Alex sat on the cold cement floor with her back against the rear tire and quietly cried her own tears, the only tears she could remember crying.

Frances returned and gave Spunky a shot that calmed him. He no longer seemed to be in pain. Aunt Edie came into the room and asked for a moment alone. As much of a fuss as she made about Spunky's destructive behavior, she loved him and told him as much. She gave him orders to "Leave the flowerbeds alone when he got to Heaven".

Alex's turn was next and the adults moved to the corner to give her some privacy. Uncle George left the small room completely. Alex looked into her friend's now calm eyes and told him stories about how they would see each other again someday and about how happy he had made her. Spunky's eyebrows moved up and down as Alex spoke but he seemed too relaxed to do much else. She hugged him and began violently crying which caused the adults to cry as well.

Almost 3 hours passed and the sun began to set. Frances mentioned to George that the sedatives would be wearing off soon and that Spunky's returning pain would be torturous. He walked over to Alex, who was still slumped over her ailing dog.

"Alex, honey, it's time. I don't want to take him away, but I have to. I am so sorry, but we have to say our final goodbyes to Spunky," her uncle said, choking back tears.

Alex stood and pretended not to see the small .22 caliber pistol that Uncle George was trying to hide behind his back. She ran to her aunt as Uncle George gingerly slid his arms under Spunky and lifted him from the table. He carried the family pet past the three females and out the side door. Spunky looked back at Alex as his head hung over the side of George's arm. The look of fear and confusion in his eyes would stay with Alex for as long as she could remember. It was something she saw in nightmares for years, only to be joined by other, equally painful sights.

Aunt Edie led Alex back into the house, an arm draped lovingly across her back. Alex looked over her shoulders and saw the shadowy forms of her uncle and dog disappear into the wooded area at the end of their perfectly manicured lawn. As they passed his empty house and run, a whimper from Spunky was distinctly audible. It was the last sound he would ever make.

Nearly a minute later, a single muffled popping sound echoed in the distance. Uncle George returned to his garage for a shovel, only to disappear back into the darkness. He spent the next few hours preparing Spunky's grave-digging the hole, burying him and surrounding it with stones. Before the night was out, he would carve a wooden marker for the grave and coat it in a waterproof lacquer.

Alex didn't see any of these things that her uncle lovingly did that evening. She was in her room, on the same rug that she had been sitting on and playing with Spunky on the day of her mother's funeral. She would cry herself to sleep on that braided rug on this painful evening. The tears that so freely flowed for the loss of her friend would be the last tears she would shed out of sadness for the next five years. That future moment of weakness and self-pity would be the singular breakdown until the worst moment of her life occurred, shortly after her high school graduation.

<u>Age 16</u>

Alex wiped her hand against her jeans as she walked out of the Art Room and into the hallway. Light brown clumps of ceramics clay crumpled and rolled into balls on the paint-and-clay-splattered denim before falling to the cheap white and grey speckled tile of the hallway floor. A few more chunks of the drying clay were crusting together on the loose white strands of cloth that stuck out from around the tears above her knees. Many other high schoolers paid extravagant amounts of money for faded jeans with premade tears, but Alex's came the old fashioned way, from constant use and frequent inadvertent contact with the edge of the rapidly spinning pottery wheel.

The long buzz of the school bell marked the end of period five, simultaneously ending her favorite time of the school day and beginning her least. Period five was her free period and came right after her lunch break. She usually spent both of them in the Art classroom, alternating between bites of whatever lunch Aunt Edie had packed and brush strokes, charcoal drawings, or spins of the wheel. She could always lose herself in the work and at the same time find a happiness that she rarely, if ever, felt otherwise.

The three minutes between the bell ending period five and the second bell that started the sixth were the most torturous minutes of her day. Gym class, or Physical Education as it was listed on her report card, came next and the anticipation of being forced to interact with anyone, let alone several of the girls who were overtly rude to her, filled Alex with anxiety. Her heart pounded harder with every step she took. A cold sweat broke out across her forehead when she saw the blue metal double doors that led into the gym.

Alex always looked at her feet as she shuffled along the outside edge of the large open room. Even as she stared straight down, she would scan the room with her peripheral vision to look for any sign of "them". She almost preferred to see them in the main room, because that meant that she would not encounter "them" in the locker room.

Alex reached the far end of the gym floor and walked into the girls' locker room. She still hadn't seen any of the four girls that she was hoping to avoid, but there was plenty of time for that. The oversized white dry erase board had the words "Swim attire" written on it. Alex's racing heart sank even further. She hated swim days. She didn't like any of the sports in general, but the pool also required her to wear a school-issued bathing suit. Not only was it unflattering, but it was very tight and left little to the imagination.

Alex's dislike of skimpy clothing didn't come from poor body image or being overweight—quite the contrary. She now stood around 5 foot 10 and the hours of using her legs to push the heavy stone pottery wheel and her arms forming mounds of clay into works of beauty had shaved nearly all body fat off of her. The main reason for her shyness was because she started developing her curvy figure a bit earlier than the other girls in her class and she still hadn't stopped. Her large but perky breasts had been a magnet for stares from the boys in her school, as well as many of their fathers.

Alex hated the constant looks and ogling, and had taken to wearing clothes that hid her body. Baggy tee shirts, large men's flannels, and sweatshirts had become her normal attire. She even bought gym clothes that were two sizes too big for her, but the swim days were a different story. She had to wear the swimsuit. That always lead to stares from the boys and comments from the girls, and these interactions would continue for the next day or so.

The saddest part to Alex was that she loved to swim and enjoyed her time in the pool. She just preferred to do it when no one else was around. She was down to two choices. She could either change into the swimsuit to participate or she could try to lie her way out of it. She chose the latter. She walked over to her teacher who was leaning against the concrete wall, with arms crossed and a whistle hanging from a lanyard around her neck.

"Excuse me, Mrs. Adams," she said in a soft yet polite voice.

"Yes, what can I do for you, Miller?" the teacher asked without looking at Alex.

"I, ummm, I am having, you know, some personal issues," Alex responded, acting as embarrassed as she could muster.

"You know the rules, no blood in the pool. Change into sweats and run laps. It's just me here today so you will have to run around the side of the pool, got me?" Mrs. Adams instructed.

"Yes ma'am. I will change up," Alex said as she turned and went back to her locker.

Five minutes later, she was in her sweats and running laps just outside of the wet surface around the pool. She was one of a half dozen other girls who were doing the same. She made the mistake of looking at the side walls when turning one of the corners and paid the price when a foot shot out into her path causing her to fall awkwardly onto the rough, pebble-like surface.

"Watch where you are going, spazz," another girl said while several laughing voices filled the air.

Alex knew who it was without looking, but she did anyway. Toni, her former only friend was staring down at her. They went their separate ways after the tragic death of Spunky. Alex never really replaced her with anyone else. She had a couple of friends, but none that she allowed to get as close to her as Toni had been.

Toni had moved in a completely different direction. Her father and mother are both realtors and had managed to do quite well in the recent housing boom. They sold their house and moved to the more posh section of town where Toni's new friends lived. Braces, acne treatment, designer clothes, and lots of trips to the hair salon and nail shop later, Toni fit right in with the snobby popular crowd. She was now a cheerleader, but that was only for appearances. She was still the horribly-uncoordinated girl that Alex once knew; she just hid it under a new look.

The tripping was nothing new either. Alex had gotten used to the daily taunts, being pushed, shoved, and knocked down. Toni and her three best friends made bullying into a sport. They were cruel and ruthless. Toni in particular had zeroed in on Alex. It felt like she was trying to punish Alex for reminding her of a time when she was not the popular girl that she had turned into.

Alex stood and started running again. Her knee and wrist were now throbbing, but she refused to let Toni get the best of her. She could feel Toni's cold stare as she finished another lap. Toni had just taken her turn in the pool and was standing on the side of the pool nearest the deep end, waiting in line for her turn to dive again. Alex didn't notice her until she heard her voice again.

"Hey Alexandra, watch where you are going this time," Toni yelled as she stood, dripping wet on the opposite side of the pool. "We wouldn't want you to end up like Spunky, now would we?"

Alex's blood ran cold and boiled at the same time. She had dealt with years of this abuse from Toni and brushed it off, but Toni had never mentioned Spunky. That was the line she never should have crossed.

Toni's friends continued to laugh as Alex turned the final corner before reaching Toni. Instead of making the sharp turn that she had been making, she ran past the edge of the pool for another 15 or 20 feet before turning to look directly at Toni.

"What are you looking at, freak?" Toni challenged.

Alex didn't respond, at least not with words. She leaned forward like a football linebacker waiting for the ball to be snapped. Also like the linebacker, she charged toward her target with a single mission—to cause pain.

Toni stood, frozen by her own surprise at Alex's reaction, before trying to get out of the path of the former friend who was barreling toward her. She was too late. Her friends were not expecting to have to move either, and she banged into them as she attempted to escape. It didn't work.

Alex's shoulder collided with the right side of Toni's ribs as the friend-turned-bully tried to crouch. Two of Toni's friends were knocked to the floor by the impact, but Toni and Alex landed in a much softer place, the deep end of the pool.

When Alex opened her eyes, she saw that she was above Toni and that she still had her arms around her one-time best friend. She looked into Toni's eyes and didn't see a single trace of the girl who used to be too scared to sleep on the floor when she stayed at Alex's, always ending up cuddled next to her. No, these were the eyes of the girl who tormented her every day.

Alex also noticed something else about Toni's eyes, other than the tons of makeup that were now dissolving away. She saw fear. It was the same fear that her mother had shown. It was the same look she last saw in Spunky's eyes. Toni was afraid that she was going to die.

A wave of excitement shot through Alex's body. An electrified tingle is how she would later describe it. She was the reason that Toni feared for her life, and Alex loved it. This was a feeling that she had never felt before. Intense but satisfying, she never wanted it to end.

Toni tried desperately to break Alex's grip, but she wouldn't allow it. Toni thrashed against Alex's near superhuman rush of adrenaline to no avail. Bubbles trickled from the corners of Toni's mouth. She needed air. For that matter, so did Alex. Her lungs burned from the lack of oxygen, but she couldn't give in. Her heart pounded from the new-found, twisted joy. She was never going to let go.

Toni's thrashing grew more frantic, but also weaker. The thought of her adversary succumbing to Alex's power only added to the thrill. Alex struggled to ignore the intense burning. She needed to breathe soon, but she could not let go. The sounds of shouts outside the water alerted Alex that her time was almost up. Loud splashes from people jumping in to help boomed around her. Her need for fresh air overwhelmed her, but then Toni opened her mouth to scream and went limp. Alex smiled as everything went black.

* * * * *

Loud, barely distinguishable voices rattled off the walls of Principal Shaw's office. Alex leaned back in her hard plastic chair, resting her head against the wall outside the impromptu war room. She closed her eyes as the battle raged on, just feet away. She could feel Toni's stares burning a hole through her. A smile crept across her face as the memory of Toni's terrified face filled the darkness of her mind.

"What are you smiling about, bitch," Toni snarled.

Alex opened her eyes and locked them on Toni's, "I keep seeing what you looked like when I held you under the water. I want you to remember what it felt like to look up at me while you couldn't breathe, while you struggled to get away from me and weren't able. I want you to remember that the ONLY reason you are breathing right now is that I allow it. If you ever fuck with me again or even say Spunky's name, I will find you and watch you take your last breaths. I will stare into your eyes as the light leaves them and only the darkness remains. From now on, think of me as your own personal God."

Toni's mouth opened wider and wider but no words came out. She sat in her chair in stunned silence, too afraid to speak. Alex closed her eyes again and listened to the yelling behind her.

"I know everyone is upset, but I need you all to calm down," Principal Shaw said, attempting to reason with the four adults in his office. He sat behind his desk, as uncomfortable as he could remember being during his first year as principal.

"Calm down? That little psychopath didn't just try to kill your daughter, did she? What kind of school are you running here?" Toni's mother snapped.

"Call her that one more time, June, and I will knock your new fake teeth down your throat," Edie said, leaning forward in her seat. After seeing June's shocked look she continued, "Wow, with all the Botox, I didn't think your eyebrows still moved."

"Edie, please compose yourself," George said quietly. He had been sitting in the confines of the small office, listening to bickering for nearly 15 minutes, and he was growing tired of the whole thing. He appeared calm to everyone else, but inside he was boiling with rage.

"No, I will not. These people are making Alex into some kind of demon here, when it was their little princess who started it all," Edie angrily whispered back.

"I would rather be raising a princess than some psycho loner," June snottily responded.

"Look, George, we have known Alex for a long time and we just think that maybe she needs some counseling to deal with her issues," Barry, Toni's father said. "We aren't blaming you. We know you are doing the best you can. It isn't your fault you had someone else's problem dropped in your lap."

That did it. The final line had been crossed in George's eyes. He slowly rose to his feet and took one methodical step toward the much younger man standing in the back of the room. George continued his advance toward Barry as he spoke in a low growl.

"Yes, Alex has had a rough life. She has been through more than any one person should have to, let alone a child. She does see a counselor and she has, ever since she watched her mother get killed in front of her. If you want to talk about problems, how about your little girl, who apparently thinks so little of herself that she has to bully other kids to make herself feel better? How about you address that? Go ahead and ask Principal Shaw if he has EVER once had a behavioral issue with Alex. Go ahead!"

Shaw answered, "No, not a one. She pretty much keeps to herself."

"Now how about your privileged little monster? How many complaints does he have about her and her clique? How many times has he seen them accost another student because of the clothes they wore, the way the spoke, or some other bullshit reason."

"It does happen a lot, Barry," Shaw responded.

"So this one time, someone stood up to her and she got what was coming to her," George said.

"Alex nearly drowned her," Barry interrupted.

"Do not talk over me. You will wait until I am done," George continued. "You want to talk about counseling? How about all the kids who your girl torments day after day? Do you know how many times I have seen Alex upset about something that was done at school, but she didn't want to say anything? Do you know how long she cried when they stopped being friends? I am done watching that girl be hurt because of yours. You straighten her out, or the next time we have this talk, it will be outside of this school. And one last thing, if you ever insult MY daughter like this again, I will do way worse to you than Alex did to Toni."

George turned and looked at his smiling wife. Without another word they left the room. As they stepped into the hallway, George looked down at Alex. She may have grown since that first day 13 years ago, but all he could see was the dirty little toddler, in need of so many things. Most of all, in need of someone to love her the way she deserved. He had loved her as his own daughter every moment since.

"Come on, honey, let's go," George said, reaching his hand out to her the same gentle way that he had handed her that blue crayon many years ago.

The three members of Alex's family rode home in silence. George fumed in the driver's seat while his wife sat next to him with a proud smile. She was just as angry as he was, but seeing George fight for Alex reminded Edie that the man she loved was the best example of a father that she had ever met.

The silence continued for the next two hours as the night sky grew dark and eventually all the lights in the Parker's home were turned off. Alex found herself unable to sleep in the ominous quiet until she saw a flash of light coming from the back side of the garage. She rose from her bed and walked, barefoot, though the house and into the back yard, where she found her uncle sitting in the same spot as she had back on the day of her mother's funeral.

"Uncle George?" Alex said quietly.

"Hey Alex, what are you doing up?" George asked in a way that was more curious than upset.

"I couldn't sleep," she answered. "I just wanted to say that I am sorry for today."

George looked up at her and patted the bench next to him. She walked over and sat down. Even though she was now taller than he was, she still felt like a little girl next to him. Hurting him or making him disappointed in her was crushing her. George put his arm around her, and she leaned her head on his shoulder.

"I don't want you to be sorry. You stood up for yourself. And I am proud of you for that. Girls like Toni, they push people around to make themselves feel better about something they don't like about themselves. It has nothing to do with you. She just thought she could get away with it, and now she knows she can't. Don't ever let anyone push you around. You are too special for that. Speak up when you know something is right, and always go after what makes you happy. Do you hear me? I mean it. You deserve to have everything you could ever want."

"Yes sir," Alex said looking at her uncle. Why couldn't everyone be like him? "Uncle George, can I ask you a question?"

"Always," he answered.

"I heard you call me your daughter," she started.

"I'm sorry, Alex. That wasn't fair of me. I know you have a real father and I'm not him. I just can't help but look at you that way. I don't mean any disrespect to your mom and dad," George said, looking at his feet.

"Would you?" Alex asked.

"Would I what?" George asked as he turned to look at Alex. He found her tear filled green eyes staring back at him.

"Be my Dad—would you and Aunt Edie adopt me?" Alex asked, turning away as a tear fell from her tilted head, splashing on her thigh. "I understand if you don't want to, or if you need to talk to Aunt Edie."

George placed a single finger under her chin and titled her head back up to face his. Alex saw his eyes welling with tears of his own. "I don't need to talk to your Aunt Edie. I know she would say the same thing that I will. We love you like a daughter. We always have, and we will until the world ceases to be. To us, you already are our daughter, and if you would like to make it official, we will go to the courthouse on Monday and drop off the paperwork."

Alex smiled and said. "I want to be a Parker. I want to be your daughter. Wait, don't you need to get the paperwork first?"

"No, I've had it waiting in case this day ever came. Nothing would make this old man happier. Let's go wake Aunt Edie."

"Can I call you Dad?" Alex asked.

George was too emotional to talk. He just stood and hugged her whispering, "I love you, Alexandra Parker."

She squeezed him tightly and whispered back, "I love you too, Daddy."

Freshman Year: Age 18

"Hey there Dad, it's Alex...again. I know you said it was nothing, but I really think you should get that stomach ache checked out. You're no spring chicken, you know. I am sure you are just looking at your cell and trying to figure out how to check your messages, but call me back, please," Alex said, as she left a fourth message on George's phone since she had woken up a few hours prior.

Alex was just about to leave another message on Edie's phone when she noticed that she was almost late for her life drawing class. Normally, she walked into the classroom on the second floor of the Maine College of Art— MECA as it was known to most people—and wondered what man or woman would be walking onto the large circular platform in the center of the room and dropping their robe.

It wasn't the complete nudity of the subject that she enjoyed as much as the fact that she was really good at drawing the contours of the human body. It was actually one of the repeating themes in her nearly nightly calls home. She could picture George and Edie squirming uncomfortably while she discussed the naked person she had just drawn. They always told her how proud they were, and she knew they meant it.

Her first semester, the previous fall, had been a feeling-out process in and of itself. Portland was the first city, by Maine standards, that she had spent any time in by herself. Hell, she had never seen a crosswalk before that had lights directing you. Portland only has about 70,000 full time residents, but many of the 300,000 who live in the surrounding communities traveled there for work or pleasure. Just living in an apartment was a huge adjustment.

The best part of her new life was the people. She spent her days surrounded by artists, an eclectic group of people who were much like she was. Many were also on the outside of the high school cliques, but here they flourished. She had more friends than she could count. Nearly every face was a friendly one, from the other students, to the professors, to the owners of the art supply shops that she frequented for her needs.

She had even chosen to spend most of her winter break at school rather than going home. She did visit with her family for the holidays, and even her extended family and cousins all commented on how much happier she seemed. Life was going so well for Alex that she couldn't imagine returning to the infinite sadness that she had felt in high school. That was, until she talked to George the night before.

She had been very excited to share news about her paintings and ceramics being included in the spring alumni and students show. She was hoping to sell enough of it and maybe have a few pieces commissioned so she wouldn't have to work a summer job. She chatted away without taking a breath for at least a minute and a half before she realized that something was off. She asked him what was wrong, and he told her that he had been having a strange pain in his stomach all day and that it was getting tough to breathe.

Alex told him to go see the doctor, and he assured her that if he didn't feel better in the morning, he would go see someone. For the first time since she had left home to go to school, he ended the call on his own. No matter how tired he had been in the past, or even if she forgot and called him while he was watching football, he always stayed on until she was out of things to say. Not last night. He ended with his usual "I love you and am proud of you", but didn't have much more to say. She had worried all night, and now she was starting to freak out.

As class ended, she reached into her handmade denim messenger bag that held most of her day-to-day necessities. She bought it from her upstairs neighbor who made them as a hobby. It was one of her best purchases to date. Pulling out her dirty phone from the bottom of the cavernous bag, the screen showed four missed calls from Mom and one voicemail. Alex hit the voicemail button and was most of the way down the stairs before Edie's voice began.

"I got her voicemail again. I think she is in class, but I don't have her schedule with me," Edie said to some unknown person before realizing that the message was recording. "Hey honey, it's Mom. Dad went to the doctor's office this morning and they decided to send him to Bangor for some tests. It's probably nothing. His stomach ache is now hurting his back, so he probably has kidney stones. I will let you know when we know what is going on. Love you."

Alex burst through the doors and onto the cool sidewalk of Congress Street. At this time of morning, the sun was still behind the building and left her side of the street cool and crisp while the other side of Congress was sunny and at least ten degrees warmer. The badly hidden worry in Edie's voice made her even more worried than she had been. She returned the call twice but immediately heard her mom's voice on her voicemail. She only shut her phone off when she was at a hospital or church, increasing the worry.

A few minutes later, Alex retrieved her car from the long-term parking garage where she stored it and started the two-hour, anxiety-filled drive to Bangor. Terrified thoughts about losing the man she now called "Daddy" intermixed with beautiful memories. One of the happiest was when she stood next to George and Edie and told the judge that she wanted to be formally adopted and change her name to Alexandra Parker. Even now, as she sped her way through the last few miles of Interstate 95 and the streets leading to Eastern Maine Medical, that vision made her smile.

Alex pulled into the visitor parking lot and started running. The door to her car didn't completely close, but she didn't care. By the time it latched, she was already a half dozen parking spots away and not looking back. She dodged other pedestrians, slow walkers, and people being pushed in wheelchairs, zigging and zagging around every obstacle while tossing out the occasional obligatory "excuse me".

The automatic sliding entrance doors of the ground floor were nearly closed when she reached them, but that didn't slow her down. Alex dove in sideways, barely grazing the rubber seals on the edges. She stumbled through a second set of doors and finally reached the information desk.

"I am looking for George Parker," she panted, out of breath with her hands resting on the desk. The woman sitting behind the desk, who hadn't even had a chance to ask Alex how she could help, searched the directory.

"Family or friend?" the woman asked politely.

"Daughter," Alex responded, her lungs working to catch up to the unexpected cardio workout.

"I show him being in surgery. There is a waiting room on the second floor. Do you know where it is?" the woman asked, but it was too late. Alex was already dashing toward the stairs.

The truth was that she had no idea where the waiting room was. As soon as she reached the top of the stairs, she began searching for a sign to direct her. When that didn't work, she began asking the people around her and was pointed down a hallway on the left.

A quick run and several turns later, she spotted Edie, pacing back and forth in front of a room marked "Surgical Waiting Room". Alex ran to her and hugged her.

"Alex, when did you get here?" she asked.

"I got your message, so I jumped in the car. I tried calling you back," Alex answered.

"Oh, I shut it off to save the battery. You didn't need to come, but I am glad you did," Edie said, hugging Alex again.

"Mom, how is Dad doing? Why is he in surgery?" Alex asked.

"Well, let's go sit and talk," Edie said as she led Alex into the nearly empty waiting room.

"Okay, you are worrying me," Alex said, taking an empty chair next to Edie and turning sideways to face her.

"I am worried, too, dear. He woke up yesterday with some pressure and pain in his stomach. I told him to go to the doctor, but you know how he is. He just said that he was getting old and took some antacids. He took a nap, but he felt worse after," Edie said looking at the floor.

"Yeah, he didn't sound so good when we talked last night," Alex said quietly.

"I told him to go to the doctor again. I kept reminding him about the heart attacks and back surgeries that he has already had, but he was stubborn. Told me that I worry too much. By the time he figured he should be seen, the office was closed and he wouldn't go to the hospital," Edie continued.

"He told me he would go today, but I wanted him to go last night," Alex said.

"Well, this morning his back was aching, he had some stuff that looked like bruises, and his stomach seemed really tight. He wasn't breathing very well, so he went to the clinic. They told him that he needed to go to the hospital and the ambulance picked him up there. He had some scans done when he got here, and when I got here they said he had a tear in his aorta that was leaking blood into his abdomen. They took him in for surgery three hours ago."

"Did you see him before they took him in? How was he?" Alex asked.

"No, they said he had to go in right away. The last time I saw him was when he left to go to the doctor's this morning," Edie answered.

Edie stopped talking and stared through the glass wall, and Alex turned to see what she was looking at. A man in blue scrubs walked into the room and stopped in front of their chairs.

"Mrs. Parker, my name is Dr. Owens and I have been operating on your husband," the tall skinny man said before looking quizzically at Alex.

"She is our daughter, Alex," Edie said, answering the unasked question. "You can tell me whatever you need to in front of her."

"Okay," Dr. Owens said with a nod. His face became more solemn as he spoke. "When we opened up Mr. Parker, we found a sizable rupture to his aorta, the main artery that takes blood from your heart and sends it to the rest of your body. It appears as though the rupture happened at least 24 hours ago, and as a result he has lost a lot of blood. It also means that many of his organs haven't been getting the blood that they need and have been damaged as a result."

"But you were able to fix that, right?" Alex asked, hoping that the answer was going to be positive.

"Yes and no," the surgeon answered. "We stopped the bleeding and repaired the tear, but the aorta itself isn't in great shape. We could do a replacement surgery, but because of the blood loss and tissue damage, he is too weak to attempt another surgery. We are giving him a transfusion right now and hope that it will help, but his blood pressure is very low. If his heart isn't able to rebound and help get the new blood to the organs, there won't be anything more we can do."

"He is really strong. He can get better. I know he can," Alex said, as much to herself as to anyone else.

"At his age and with his cardiac issues, I am not sure that he will recover. I'm sorry. I wish I had better news, but the next hour is critical," Dr. Owens said.

"Can we see him?" Edie asked.

"He is still in ICU recovery and isn't awake yet. I think we should let him rest for a bit, but as soon as you can see him, someone will come and get you."

"Thank you, Doctor," Edie said and the surgeon left the room.

Alex and Edie sat in near silence for the next 30 minutes or more. Neither noticed how long it had been, nor did they make the effort to speak. Each was running over what the surgeon had just told them in the chaos of their own minds.

Edie saw visions of the man she fell in love with, a young George in his Navy uniform before he shipped out to fight in WWII. She saw him on the day he returned, and then again on their wedding day, standing in a field behind her parents' home while family and friends looked on at two young kids with their lives ahead of them. She saw his face as she cried and told him that her doctor had told her she couldn't have children, dashing their hopes for a huge family. She remembered how he cried too, but told her that no matter whether they had children or not, he would always be happy. She made him better in his own eyes, and it didn't matter if they had children or not.

Edie thought about the holidays, the vacations, the fun, and the arguments. She remembered the day that they found Alex, and the other moments of their lives since. She saw the two of them standing in the back yard while he showed Alex how to paint his birdhouses. She saw how happy he was when they adopted her, and the excitement on his face when she called each day. She saw the pride with which he showed off Alex's artwork, the paintings that filled their walls, and the cups and pots that she had made. He drank his coffee from the first mug Alex ever made, misshapen as it was. He had been the best partner that Edie could have hoped for, and now he might be taken from her.

Alex's mind was also filled with thoughts of George. She remembered him always being in the background for the big moments in her life. She had a fuzzy memory of the day they met and every moment since. He had become more than a father figure. He was supportive in everything she did, but told her when she was wrong. He let her make mistakes and fall down so she could learn when all he wanted to do was catch her and protect her. He never said so, but she felt it. He was the one who taught her to ride her bike. He spent hours in the driveway with her, holding her up while she tried to pedal. He was the person who picked her up when she fell in the ditch or ran ahead to stop her from going in the road. He took care of Spunky in his last moments and he alone handled the toughest parts. He was more than a father. He was a friend—the best she had ever had, and now she was losing him.

"Mrs. Parker?" a nurse asked, interrupting the two women who meant the most to George while they each thought about how he was the most important person in their lives.

"Yes, that is me," Edie said, feeling the need to stand.

"I am so sorry. His pressure just isn't rising. He isn't responding to the treatment. I hate to tell you this, but it is time to say goodbye," the nurse said.

The room started spinning and Alex felt like she couldn't breathe. That couldn't be right. There was always something that could be done, right?

"If you follow me, I will take you to him," the nurse said, and the women followed. Once they reached the ICU, the nurse spoke again. "He is in bed six. He is still unconscious, but you can talk to him. I am so sorry."

Everything seemed like it was moving in slow motion. Alex felt like she was in some surreal movie version of her life but was watching it happen rather than actually being in control. She saw herself moving closer to George's bed but didn't think she was the one moving. She watched as Edie leaned over and whispered to him, kissing him on the forehead before returning to Alex with tears falling down her reddened cheeks.

"It is your turn, if you want to talk to him. I think he would understand if you couldn't," Edie said to Alex.

She didn't respond—she just started moving closer and closer. She looked down at her father and couldn't believe what she saw. For the first time in her life, he looked old and fragile. He had an IV inserted into wrinkled, paper-thin skin. The hospital gown made him look gaunt and sickly. She didn't like this at all. The machines next to his bed made sporadic beeps and other noises, and she could feel the oxygen from his nasal cannulas overflowing around his nostrils. This couldn't be her Daddy.

Alex grabbed George's hand and was surprised by how cold it felt. His hands were always chilly and he blamed his "poor circulation" for it, but this was different. It scared her even more. She looked down at his ghostlike face and closed eyes, not sure if he would hear her, but she spoke anyway.

"Daddy, it's me, Alex. I am here. I want you know that I love you," she started, trying to sound mature and strong, but that soon fell apart. "They said you aren't going to make it, but I know they are wrong. You are stronger than that. You can make it; I know you can. I need you to."

Tears formed in the corners of her eyes and spilled out onto her cheeks. The spreading warmth made everything feel more real. She switched from talking to a panicked begging. "I need you to make it, Dad. I love you. I can't do this without you. I need you to get better. You have to be at my graduation. I need you to walk me down the aisle. Who will I dance with if you aren't there? Please! Don't go. Mom and I need you. You can do it. Just start trying. I will quit school and stay home. I won't go away again. Please, just get better."

The beeping became more erratic and an alarm sounded. She looked up at the monitor and saw that his blood pressure, heart rate, and oxygen levels were dropping. She screamed, "Someone help us!"

A doctor calmly walked over to the other side of the bed. He reached up and turned off the monitor to save everyone the sound of the imminent flat lining. "I am sorry. There is nothing more we can do."

"Daddy, you need to fight! Come on, try. Please, please, please. Please God, take someone else. He is too good to take. He has too much left to do here!" Alex begged both George and a God she didn't believe in.

"Come on, honey, he's gone," Edie said, her arms on Alex's shoulders, pulling her back.

"No, I have to give him a hug," Alex said, shaking her mother's hands off of her. She leaned in closer and kissed her father's forehead and then hugged him gently. "I love you, Daddy. I am going to miss you. You are the best thing that ever happened to me."

Edie pulled her hysterical daughter away, fighting the same feelings inside. She knew she had to be the strong one now. She was used to setting the rules and enforcing them—being the bad guy when necessary. She hugged her daughter and looked over Alex's shoulder as George's life ended.

Alex struggled through the next few hours and then days. Nothing seemed the same as it was before. Everything felt darker, emptier, like something was missing. Something was missing—her father, her lighthouse in every storm of her life. She was facing the biggest one now and he was gone. How would she survive without him? He left a void in her heart that could never be filled, and at that moment, she decided that no one would ever have the chance to try. She would not let anyone be that close again.

Age 20: Alex's First Kill

A hand waved into Alex's field of vision, between her nose and the small lump of clay she was slowly trying to form into a handleless tea cup to finish off another set. What started off as a mistake a few months prior had turned into her biggest seller. When the handles fell off of two of her tea cups, she sanded down the rough edges and tried to sell them as Asian inspired tea bowls, and this design had really caught on with the area's many hipsters.

Alex removed her ear buds, but could still hear the music calling her back. She found that heavier rock really helped her work out the building aggression and sufficiently blocked out the noise around her. She looked up to see the source of her disruption and found Noel standing just inside her "studio". The studios were a specific work space for each art student to use once they had chosen their major. Alex was doing a double major of painting and ceramics and had two spaces, but she was usually in her small wooden ceramics cubicle.

"Hey Alex, are you going to be here for a while?" Noel asked as he swiped at a loose chunk of unruly bangs that frequently fell across his eyes.

"I think so, what's up?" Alex asked, knowing the answer before he said it. It was Friday night and he was scheduled to watch the school's kilns to make sure there weren't any issues. It was a required job that everyone had to do at some point, but that he always seemed to get out of.

"Umm, well, I was hoping you could take part of my shift tonight. I totally forgot that I promised Maya that I would meet her for dinner. I shouldn't be gone long," he said. They both knew it was a lie, but Alex pretended otherwise.

"I will be here until 11. Can you be back by then or find someone else?" Alex said. She knew that she would be there all night regardless of what Noel said. She just wanted to be able to go back to him when she needed something and be able to remind him of when he bailed and she covered.

"Yeah, totally, we are just getting dinner and maybe a drink or two. I will let Dr. Wilde know that you are covering for a bit," Noel said, disappearing back through the curtain entryway of her cubicle before he finished speaking.

Dr. Wilde would undoubtedly be happy to hear about the switch. He was the faculty staff member on site for the night, basically hanging around to make sure the students didn't burn the place down. Other professors chilled in their offices, worked on their own pieces, or slept, but not Wilde. He was known for cruising the floors after the security guard locked the public access doors at 9 PM, looking for a co-ed to talk to.

Dr. Wilde was a favorite amongst most of his students. At 36, he was one of the younger faculty members, and many students found it easy to both look up to him for his commercial success and see him as a peer. He purposely tread the line between friend and authority figure, taking joy in crushing the egos of some of the more cocky males while feasting on the females, particularly the ones with "daddy issues".

On paper, Alex was an ideal target for Dr. Wilde. She was young, gorgeous, shy, had no contact with her biological father, and the only father she had ever known was now deceased. It didn't hurt that she found Wilde to be attractive. She enjoyed his attention, but didn't have any interest in being another co-ed conquest.

After a brief run to grab some Pad Thai, Alex returned to the ceramic wing and stopped into the kiln room. Predictably, Noel's name was scratched out and Alex's was written on the schedule in its place. A few other people were milling around the large room. A handful of upperclassmen gently placed various pieces of still-soft clay into the large freestanding hexagonal and octagonal kilns around the perimeter walls. They sealed the kilns shut and set the temperature and timers. They were going the "idiot proof" route and would be back in the morning to unload their freshly fire-hardened work to later be glazed various colors and refired.

Thankfully, those kilns were not Alex's job tonight. Those pieces were fully the responsibility of the person who signed out the kiln. Unlike the work of the underclassmen, who normally struggled just to complete their assignment pieces, many of the pieces in the solo kilns were commissioned works or other work that would be sold.

Alex's job tonight would be to control the huge walk-in industrial-sized kiln that took up the entire back wall of the room.

Alex looked at the shelves inside the walls of the kiln as well as the several pedestals in the open floor area. She had plenty of room left to put the forty or so pieces that were sitting on the "to be loaded shelf" into the space. Each piece was supposed to have an identifying mark on the bottom to show which artist it belonged to. If it didn't, it wouldn't go in. Alex would arrange the various pieces on the shelves in such a way that each had enough room so none touched. If a piece was too sloppily made or the clay was too soupy, causing it to droop, it would be left out. If they had obvious air/water bubbles, they were also left out. Bubbles lead to the piece cracking or exploding, and usually damaging other neighboring works.

Alex had about an hour's worth of work ahead of her, so she planned to eat her dinner and return in 45 minutes to have plenty of time. She also needed to get the wood and coal chunks ready to feed into the furnace that supplied the heat for the kiln. Since they were all using red clay to make their pottery, Alex was going to be trying to keep the internal temperature around 1500-1800 degrees. She would be loading the fuel sources into the hopper, which fed the furnace. She had to watch the temperature gauges and work the oxygen feeding lever. More oxygen meant higher temperatures. Because the gauges were notoriously unreliable, she also needed to put on welder's goggles every 15 or 20 minutes to look inside the kiln itself.

She would only need to remove the brick that blocked the viewing port for a few seconds to look at the colors in the room.

Alex returned to her studio to eat and relax before starting her shift. Tiredness and fatigue spread through her mind and muscles. She closed her eyes, balanced the aluminum take-out container on her thighs, and wondered why she agreed to take the shift in the first place. She didn't even like Noel or his girlfriend, Maya.

"Asleep on the job already?" a familiar voice said, startling her.

Alex opened her eyes and saw Dr. Wilde standing inside the room. He smiled at her and didn't even attempt to hide his gaze, which was focused squarely down the front of the rounded, low-slung neck of the men's tank top style tee shirt she wore while working. She always put on coveralls so she didn't ruin her own clothes, and an apron over that, but at this moment she was sitting with the apron off and the coveralls down around her waist. *Do you know that you are a completely predictable cliché, Dr. Wilde?* She thought to herself.

"No, just taking a break before the fun starts. I wasn't supposed to be scheduled, so I am not totally prepared to stay up all night," Alex said.

"It was nice of you to cover for Noel. I am surprised you said that you would on such short notice," Dr. Wilde said.

"Why?" Alex asked.

"I just figured that a pretty girl like you would have plans on a Friday night, is all," Wilde responded.

"Nope, no plans," Alex said.

"No special person? No boyfriend or girlfriend or both?" Wilde said, stepping closer.

"No, not really," Alex said, standing to create some distance.

"I can't believe that. Guys must be lining up," Wilde said, closing the gap.

"I've been out a few times, but nothing really stuck. I just haven't found someone that I have enough in common with," Alex said, stepping back a half step. She felt the back wall touching her shoulders and the bench digging into her knees. She was out of real estate. She needed to end this conversation soon or who knows what would happen. For some unknown reason, she didn't move.

"I think I know the reason," Wilde said, brushing a strand of hair behind her right ear. Alex could smell the combination of sweat and cologne on his skin, and she liked it—musky and manly. "I have always thought that you were more mature than your age—an old soul. Old souls see the world differently and have a tougher time connecting with these young boys. A woman like you needs a more mature man, someone who knows what he wants....and takes it."

Dr. Wilde leaned in closer and brushed his lips against hers. A tingle shot down her spine. She didn't think she was interested in him, but she hadn't been kissed like this in a while. She kissed back, putting her hand on the back of his head. He kissed her softly at first, but quickly it became harder, more intense. His hands reached for her, at first they rested on her hips but then they moved north towards her breasts. She almost stopped them as they crossed her stomach, but she didn't. She lowered her hand back down and tried to relax.

Only a few seconds later, his hands began roaming again. This time they moved to the last shoulder strap of her coveralls, unsnapping them and pushing them to the side. His right hand grazed her breast again on its way lower. It stopped at the bottom of her shirt, but only momentarily. She felt his fingers on her bare stomach and flinched. As the hand slid further up her shirt she stopped the kiss and pushed him away.

"What is wrong? Is it not private enough? Are you worried that someone will walk in? I get it. How about you meet me in my office?" Wilde said, his words pushing the limits, just as his hands had.

"No, I think I just don't want to do anything. I am sorry," Alex said.

"Sorry? You should be sorry. Do you realize what you do to a guy when you lead him on like this?" Wilde said, his demeanor changing.

"I didn't lead you on. You came on to me," Alex said.

"I think you just got scared and need to relax," Wilde said, leaning in again.

"I don't think so," Alex said as she pushed him away and walked around him. "I've got to go."

"No, you have plenty of time. Come back and we can talk about this," Wilde said, grabbing her wrist.

"Leave me alone," Alex said, pulling her hand away and walking out of the studio.

"Come back here, you fucking tease," Wilde said, chasing after her.

Alex ran down the hall and into the kiln room where thankfully, several other students were still hanging around and talking. Dr. Wilde stopped at the entrance and upon seeing the other students, kept walking.

Shaken but okay, Alex focused on loading the kiln, and before she knew it the job was almost done. The last of the other students had left ten minutes ago, and she was now alone. Well, she thought she was alone.

Just as Alex placed the last bowl on the shelf, a pair of hands slid across her body from behind. The hands moved under her coveralls and came to rest, cupping her breasts again. She felt lips kissing her neck and heard Wilde whisper, "I thought they would never leave."

Alex pulled away from her professor and said, "I said that I am not interested. Leave me alone, or I am calling security."

"Oh, don't be like that. I know you are nervous, but I promise you will like it. Let's just give it a shot and see what happens. I have some tequila in my office to take the edge off. It's exciting, isn't it?" Wilde said, stepping closer again.

"I said NO!" Alex yelled.

"You don't get to say no to me," Wilde said. "I can easily go to the Dean and say you made a pass at me. Who do you think he will believe? Huh? So why don't you calm down and do what you are told?"

The friendly teacher act was long gone, replaced by the eyes of a predator. Alex didn't have any interest in being his prey. He advanced closer and grabbed at her. She slapped his hand away. A burning sensation filled her left cheek as he slapped her, hard. He stepped even closer and pushed her against the wall, pawing at her clothes. Alex yelled, but no one responded. She did the only thing she could think of, and that was to push him. She put both hands in the middle of his chest and pushed. He stepped backward, but then advanced again. Alex pushed Dr. Wilde a second time, with more force.

"I love it when you bitches put up a fight. It makes it so much more fun when you finally give it up. Don't worry, I'll be gentle...maybe," Wilde said with a crazed look in his eye.

Wilde stepped forward quickly and Alex reacted by slamming her hands into his chest. He wasn't prepared for the force behind her push and he slipped backwards, falling to the ground. Wilde tried to brace himself but he didn't see the low table behind him. His head smashed into it with an audible cracking that echoed in the chamber.

Terror washed over Alex. What could she do? Was he dead? What would happen if he reported this as an assault? She couldn't afford to switch schools. What was she going to do?

Alex thought she saw Dr. Wilde's legs move and she ran for the door. She swung the heavy doors shut and pulled out the brick that blocked the viewing port. He was still on the ground. Surprisingly, he wasn't bleeding. Alex was completely confused and scared. Then she looked to her right and saw the start button for the furnace. Without thinking, she reached over and pushed it. The furnace kicked on and the kiln room heated.

Alex continued to peer through the opening into the room as she felt the heat building. She couldn't tell if he was moving, or if the heated air was playing tricks with her mind. She thought he groaned, and she reacted by opening the air valve, increasing the heat to 300 degrees. She put the brick back and watched the temperature gauge as it rose steadily—350, 400, 500, he couldn't be alive at this point. The temperature rose and rose until it settled at 1650 degrees, well above what was necessary to dry and burn flesh before reducing it to dust.

Six hours later, the kiln had finished its cycle and was in the process of cooling down when Alex took a second look into the cavern. Her would-be rapist was no longer recognizable as anything. He had been reduced to a pile of ash and a few very charred bone fragments, along with a dried puddle of what fat he had covering his body. Alex opened the door and entered the cooled room. She used a dust pan to sweep up the dust and bits of bone. The kiln had reached temperatures similar to a crematorium and had been on longer, which allowed the bone to break down.

Alex closed the door and walked to the trash can. She almost threw the ashes out when she noticed the barrel that held the ash and sand that many students used to dry out over watered clay. She tipped the dustpan and dumped Dr. Wilde in with the other ash. She mixed them together and took the bits of bone to the "reject crusher", a pneumatic press that students used to crush broken or screwed up pieces of ceramics that had already been fired. The dust would be mixed in with the ash or with various colors of glazes. She placed the half dozen bone shards under the press's hammer and watched as they were pulverized.

For the first time since she threatened Toni after the "pool incident", Alex felt a surge of power. She felt invincible. She wasn't sad about killing Dr. Wilde. He had tried to rape her and had probably done it to others. She had done the world a favor, and likely saved countless other girls from facing the same proposition. Alex felt a renewed invincibility, bordering on omnipotence. She had the power to control who lived and who died, and she loved it. A single thought entered her mind…..

I want to do it again. Soon.

Two Months Later

"...and then he turned away from me. I pushed him over the railing. He screamed, but there wasn't anyone else around to hear him. The scream only lasted a second, anyway. He was dead as soon as he hit the rocks," Alex said as she sat at Edie's bedside and held her mother's bony hand between hers. She paused to wipe pureed peaches from the frail woman's chin.

"There was so much blood, Mom. I knew that I should have been leaving, but I couldn't stop staring. It was cloudy and pitch black everywhere else in the park, except for the lighthouse and the rocks below it. We were glowing in the light of the full moon. The way the waves reached out and covered his body and then pulled away, taking the blood with it, was almost....magical. I could have sworn that it was feeding off of him. I get shivers just thinking about it," Alex said. She rubbed her hands up and down on her bare arms, goose bumps rising out of the flesh as she spoke.

The white plastic spoon scraped the last of Edie's meal, the turkey, potatoes, and gravy that had been pureed and then mixed with a thickener to help keep her from aspirating as she ate. Many patients who were in the late stages of Alzheimer's or dementia had trouble eating and swallowing correctly. They also tended to get food or liquid in their lungs, causing pneumonia—a very common cause of death.

Edie had been treated for pneumonia more than a dozen times since George's passing, and judging on the crackling wheeziness that Alex heard every time her mother took a breath, it was back. The frequent dosages of antibiotics had made her almost resistant to their effect. She appeared to be weakening in Alex's opinion, but because it had been almost a year since her mother had spoken coherently, it was hard to tell. Alex liked to think that she noticed subtle cues in her unchanging expressions.

"Don't look at me like that, Mom. I am not crazy. I know it sounds bad, but he deserved it. He was a scumbag cheating on my friend and it literally took him like five minutes to hit on me when I met him. Any guy who tries to sleep with a stranger when he has a girlfriend shouldn't be allowed to breed. I did the world a favor. Besides, I am just having some fun to blow off steam. I am really stressed out about what I am going to do after I graduate, and this helps. I won't need to do it once things calm down, I promise."

Edie stared in Alex's direction, but whether she understood what Alex was saying, had an opinion about the topic, or even if she recognized Alex at all, was anyone's guess. Her decline was unexpected and quite rapid. After George's funeral, she didn't want to be alone in the home they had shared for over 40 years, so she decided to stay with her cousin and her cousin's spouse for a few days. It didn't take long for Judith, her cousin, to start noticing that something wasn't right with Edie.

The signs were subtle at first, a tea kettle forgotten on the stove until all the water had boiled away, mixing up the names of loved ones, asking a question and then asking it again an hour later, and so on. Judith and her husband, Tom, decided that it might be best for Edie to stay with them for a while longer. She frequently talked about George—mainly about him coming home soon. At first, Judith reminded her about his passing, but it began to feel cruel to make her relive the loss of the love of her life, and so she played along. He would be home soon. Should they make something special for his dinner?

Within six months, she went from merely seeming forgetful when Alex called to barely speaking at all. Judith and Tom did their best, but they were nearly 70 years old; they just didn't have the energy or strength to keep up with her needs. Edie stopped feeding herself and had to be slowly fed by hand, usually requiring more than an hour to do so. The final straw came when she started having somewhat violent reactions to Judith and Tom, who she no longer appeared to recognize.

Alex and Judith made arrangements for Edie to move into a nursing care facility that specialized in assisting people with dementia and Alzheimer's. It was close to Alex's school and the house she was renting, so they were able to spend more time together. Their daily ritual was for Alex to show up between her morning and afternoon classes with her lunch and she would feed Edie whatever the dietary nurses had prepared for her.

Because Edie was now almost completely nonverbal, Alex did the talking for both of them. The first few visits were uncomfortable and Alex struggled to figure out how to talk to her mother. Should she speak loudly or use small words? Eventually, she decided that she should just talk like she normally would have. She shared stories from her day, her classes, the projects she was working on, and she even brought some in to show her.

For Christmas, Alex made a charcoal sketch of her parents' wedding photo and framed it. The nurses loved how much attention Alex gave her ill mother and she enjoyed it as well. Some days, Alex would just show up with a large sketchbook and make drawings of her mother and the staff. Things began to change when she discovered her new skill.

Each life that Alex took gave her the same rush that she had felt the night Dr. Wolfe died. She started slowly by killing a man who she saw slapping a woman near her apartment. As he walked away, she followed him until he stopped in a quiet, darkened alleyway to get out of the wind and light a cigarette. He never saw her coming as she snuck up behind him and smashed the back of his head in with a brick. She threw the brick into the ocean on her way home and burned her blood-spattered clothes.

The thrill of the hunt mixed with the righteousness of feeling that what she was doing protected other, weaker people, caused a desire to build inside her until she could no longer suppress it. It was an itch that needed scratching. At first, the itch took a long time to reappear, but each time she scratched it, the itch returned faster and faster. Now, it was her constant companion. Her mind was always on a prior killing or on the man she wanted to kill next. These thoughts carried over into her conversations with her mother as well.

Edie's role changed from mother and friend to confidante, her room turning into Alex's private confessional. Though always discrete, Alex transitioned from speaking in generalities to very vividly detailed explanations. This particular visit was doubly special as Alex not only recounted her latest triumph over a predatory male, but she also had her next target within her sights.

"I can't even begin to explain how much I hate this guy, Mom. He has lunch in the same food court that I do, like every day, and he is always fondling some poor woman who isn't his wife," Alex started to explain. "He has this fake laugh that echoes through the whole place and makes me want to punch him in the face."

Alex paused to look at the door to make sure that they were still alone. "I saw his secretary crying in front of City Hall like 2 weeks ago, and I started talking to her. She started telling me all kinds of stories about the nasty shit...sorry Mom—I mean stuff, that he does around the office. He thinks that because he is a city councilman that he can get away with it.

"I know you are probably wondering why I am going after him, but just hold your horses and I will tell you," Alex said, attempting to joke with her mother. Edie's expression stayed the same. "The reason is really personal. You know the contest that I won to create a big installation for the city? Well, he wants to cut the funding for that and basically eliminate my project altogether. I can't let that happen."

"Alex?" said Marla, the charge nurse on Edie's floor. "I don't mean to interrupt, but the paramedics will be here in a couple minutes to take her for her chest x-ray. I need to come in and clean her up."

"No problem, Marla. I am almost done anyway," Alex answered before turning to her mother. "Anyway Mom, the short version is that he is about to become a much bigger part of my sculpture than he ever thought."

Alex stood and then bent down to kiss her mother on the forehead. Edie's breathing wheezed and crackled even louder when Alex was that close to her. She turned and walked to the door and paused. Alex took a final look at the frail shell of a woman her mother had become.

"I will see you tomorrow, Mom. I love you," Alex said as she walked out. The next day, Edie would have to be fed by Marla, just as she would the next day and every day for the rest of her life, short as it would be. The nurses would wait for Alex on each of those 12 days, but she wouldn't be back again. The itch, her constant companion, was about to seize control and it refused to share her with anyone.

* * * * *

Three missed calls & voicemails, the screen on Alex's phone lit up with the same words again and again. She didn't notice. The beat-up grey smartphone had been haphazardly tossed onto her paint-splattered, tool-covered workbench in the corner of the garage. In truth, the location of the device didn't matter. It could have been directly in front of her eyes, the LED screen lighting up with a bright yellow glow every five minutes and she wouldn't have looked at it. She was too busy scratching her itch to be aware of anything happening in the world around her.

City Councilman Rusty LaMotte had proven to be all too predictable in his habits and behavior, making him disappointingly easy prey. Surely, it would take more than pretending to bump into him at lunch; a low cut shirt, fake giggle, and some bile-inducing flirting to convince him to meet a complete stranger in a dark and secluded park late at night? No, no it didn't.

Alex smiled, remembering the look of surprise on Rusty's face upon realizing that the wine they shared on Alex's couch had been drugged. Sadly, his world had become too fuzzy for him to appreciate the irony of Alex slipping rohypnol, more commonly known as "roofies", into his wine when he had planned to do the same thing later when getting her a refill.

Rusty's nine-hour slumber had been anything but restful for Alex. Even though he only weighed 170 pounds, Rusty was extremely difficult to move. Alex tried dragging him by his wrists with very limited success. The same technique reversed, tugging on his feet, fared no better. After one full hour of trial and error, she found the right combination. She rolled him onto his back with a plastic sheet under him—the same kind she normally used to protect her clients' floors when she painted murals for extra money.

Finding that one little trick not only saved her a significant amount of effort in moving Rusty, it also protected the floors under him from any blood or other trace evidence. This became especially useful when she pulled him down the steps leading from her rented home to the attached garage. Several bleeding cuts developed when the back of his head slammed against the edges of the wooden stairs. The blood pooled on the plastic, but nowhere else.

After reaching the garage, Alex simply wrapped him up in the plastic and rolled him into the open cavity of his soon-to-be-final resting place. Hopefully, he would wake up enough before he was completely entombed so that he could catch the second irony of the night. His death chamber just happened to be the statue the city had commissioned Alex to make. The very one that he planned on cutting the funding for. Instead of killing the project, he would now become part of it, slowly rotting away inside the cement and steel, just feet away from his old office at city hall. His coworkers would walk by it daily as they entered and exited the building where so many of his acts of depravity occurred.

The sculpture itself was simple in design but complex in construction. A detailed map of the entire state covered the exterior of the lightweight but durable copper structure. It had been meticulously imprinted with each town, river, lake, and mountain. The more than 300 miles of craggy coastline alone had taken nearly 35 hours. Alex had already invested thousands of dollars from her own pocket and countless laborious hours just to get it to this point. There was no way on earth that she would allow one man to take this prestigious project away from her. The doors it would open for her career alone would have an unmeasurable impact on her life.

Rusty started to stir into consciousness, but a faint beeping was getting on Alex's nerves. It was coming from behind her. She followed it to her work bench where she saw the awaiting messages and the low battery indicator light. She recognized the numbers as having come from her Mother's nursing home. She pressed play and hoped to hear the messages before the phone died.

"Hi Alex, this is Marta calling. I just wanted to let you know that your Mom's chest x-ray showed that she does have another nasty case of pneumonia. We are giving her some strong antibiotics, but we are not hopeful after the last time."

Message two began to play, left 3 hours after the first. "Alex, it is Marta again. I don't know if you got my last message but your mother is getting worse. She is still refusing food. That makes 4 days in a row. I am hoping you can come by and maybe she will eat for you. You may need to prepare yourself to say goodbye, her oxygen levels are staying very low, even with the supplemental O2."

Seven hours later: "Ms. Parker, this is Alana Reardon. I am a Chaplin who was asked to visit with your mother, but I don't see any information about preferred last rites service or anything of the like. Could you call….."

The phone shut off, the last of its battery drained away. It felt apropos to Alex considering the messages were about her mother's life slipping away. Alex knew she should have been saddened or felt the need to rush to Edie's bedside, but she didn't. Her itch, the companion who would remain after her mother left her, told her that she needed to move on. She had a job to do and it wasn't even half done.

Alex walked back into the house and plugged her phone in to charge. When she returned to the garage, she saw Rusty struggling to sit up. His right leg draped over the edge of the copper, not quite fitting inside the cavity, but Alex had a plan to remedy that.

Alex walked over to Rusty, who stared at her with a combination of confusion and fear. He looked at his dangling leg, no doubt feeling pain as the sharp thin copper dug into the light suit pants he was wearing. "Don't worry; I am going to fix that right up,"

Rusty struggled to speak. No matter what words he chose, Alex didn't want to hear them. A dirty, polish-stained rag stuffed into his mouth did the trick. White plastic zip ties bound his wrists, leaving only the pesky leg to deal with before sealing him up. There wasn't enough room to cross his legs, one over the other but there was plenty of space available above his waist.

Alex reached above her head, her shirt lifting just enough to show an inch of midriff. Even drugged, tied up and facing death, Rusty couldn't help himself. He locked his eyes on the exposed alabaster white skin. As soon as she noticed, Alex zipped up her coveralls. "No more shows for you, asshole."

A three-foot length of chain wrapped around Rusty's ankle was then looped over the thick hook of Alex's makeshift sliding pulley. The prior renter of her house had been a mechanic, using the pulley to lift engines out of cars, and conveniently left the system up when he left. It came in handy for many of her projects, whether she had a block of stone that needed to be lifted after carving or just holding metal in place to weld.

A very beautiful feature of the pulley system was that the main block could be raised and lowered as well, allowing Alex to twist and turn heavy objects to various angles. This particular item called for the pulley to be almost parallel to the copper. Alex took her position behind the pulley and yanked down on the ropes. Rusty's leg shot straight up into the air at a nearly perfect right angle. Another tug placed his ankle halfway closer to his head. Muffled screams rang out as the pulley reached the end of its ability. Alex needed something else to finish the job.

The solution presented itself in the form of a second item abandoned by the previous renter: a weight set. One by one, the weights were threaded through the excess chain as it dangled from the pulley hook. Figuring that 75 pounds should be sufficient, she pressed the release button on the side of the mechanical pulley block and the chain dropped straight to the floor. The sudden jerk and massive pressure snapped Rusty's leg downward. Wet popping and tearing noises were audible over his muffled screams as his freshly disarticulated hip and knee joints flopped flaccidly to his chest. His right foot, complete with an Italian-made patent leather shoe that likely cost more than Alex's monthly rent, rested next to his ear.

Alex used the pulley once more, this time to lift the second half of the copper sculpture into position over the top of the first. Darkness enveloped Rusty, but just as Alex prepared to slip the straps off that held the top section in place, the doorbell rang. She lowered the top until it rested gently but precariously on its sister half and walked back into her living room, closing the garage door behind her.

A lone shadow stood on the other side of the frosted glass door. Alex rarely entertained and what few people visited her knew that she hated unannounced drop-ins. Alex opened the door slightly, until the golden chain became too taut to continue. A familiar face popped into the gap.

"Marta? What are you doing here?" Alex asked. Sure she was surprised to see her mother's nurse outside of the facility, but more than anything she was irritated by the interruption.

"I know it's early, but we haven't been able to reach you. It's about your Mom," Marta said.

"I am sorry. I have been working on a project for the city and I have been stuck on that for a few days. What's up?" Alex asked, unchaining the door and opening it. She stood in the doorway to quell any thoughts Marta may have had about coming inside.

Catching the hint, Marta responded, "Well, we were worried when we hadn't seen you for days and then no one could reach you by phone. I wanted to tell you this in person," Marta paused, tears in her eyes. "Your Mom's pneumonia got worse, the antibiotics weren't working, and she was so weak to start with…. I'm sorry but she passed away about an hour ago. I stayed and sat with her all night. I was there when she went. She just sorta dozed off and then that was it. She wasn't suffering and she didn't seem to be scared."

Alex could see that the poor woman was trying to comfort her, but all she could think about was that she had someone in the other room that *WAS* suffering and was hopefully in a lot of pain. An invisible force seemed to be pulling her back to the garage. When she didn't speak, Marta broke the silence.

"I am sure this isn't easy, even though we all knew it had to happen eventually. It never seems real. I liked your mother a lot and I would like to attend her services when you have them. I will leave you alone. I'm sure you have some grieving to do."

"Oh, yes—thank you," Alex responded. She should have been sad and grieving, but she wasn't. This had been a long time coming, and if anything she felt relieved. She was free of obligation to anyone other than herself and her new companion.

As Marta left, Alex closed and relocked her door. As soon as she saw Marta's car drive away, she reentered the garage. A final peek at Rusty's face made it evident that he was in shock. His body was waking up from the roofie-induced fog and it couldn't handle the pain from his right leg. He would shut down soon, but Alex wanted him to feel every possible second of fear and agony. Before closing the lid for the final time, she slapped him across his face to rouse him. A brief moment of clarity in his eyes followed by abject terror as the lid lowered again was all Alex needed to be satisfied. That, and knowing Rusty would still be alive for hours after she finished welding the two halves together.

For the next two hours, Rusty thrashed and did everything he could to escape his tomb, but it was all for naught. Alex finished her air- and water-tight weld, and nothing would ever enter or leave the sculpture again. Even the gases couldn't escape, and more importantly the liquids that would be created as Rusty decomposed inside the cavern would just pool in the bottom. Nothing short of cutting into the copper would ever expose Alex's secret to the light of day.

Exhaustion overtook the rush of excitement and newfound sense of freedom, and Alex closed up the wooden box that held Rusty's copper final resting place so that it could be trucked to the installation point. She shut off the lights to her garage and grabbed a box of cereal on her way to her bedroom. She discarded the dirty coveralls and stripped off the sweaty tee shirt that she wore under it. The clothing landed in a pile just outside her bedroom door.

Alex didn't bother to turn on the light as she entered her private space. It fit the literal definition of a bedroom and nothing more. The space held only a single dresser and a mattress on the floor in the far corner. She pushed the door closed behind her, but it didn't latch. It creaked slowly until it stopped at a quarter open. The early morning daylight that filled the other rooms snuck into this room, creating a triangle-shaped sliver of illuminated floor in the center.

She sat near that triangle of sunlight, her nearly naked body half-obscured by the darkness. Her bare legs rested on the cool floor, with only the small section of underwear between Alex and total nudity. She reached a dirty hand into the cereal box, the other grabbing a sketchpad. Her life had come full circle in the last seventeen-plus years. Just as she had done on the morning her parents entered her life, this morning, the day the final person on earth who she cared about left her, Alex sat on a bare floor, covered in more dirt than clothing, ate dry cereal from the box, and drew.

*Note from Author- Thank you for reading. If you would like to know more about the series that Alex is in, please turn the page. You will find the first chapter of the novel Cleansing Evil followed by a description of the same book.

Cleansing Evil (A Christian Rinaldi Thriller Book 1)

CHAPTER 1

Old onion skins and dirt. The musty scent of field dirt mixed with the skins of last year's onion crop filled Christian's nostrils and caused tears to start welling up in the corners of his eyes. The onions may have brought the tears to the surface but it was fear that was making them flow down the sides of his pudgy cheeks.

Even clear, dry eyes would have been useless to him. Darkness so complete that he was unable to see his hands in front of his face, let alone the cellar walls, enveloped him. His other senses were only marginally better in the pitch black abyss of the root cellar. When he rested his back against the cool, flaking cement, small crumbles of dirt cascaded from above, first falling onto his neck before finding their way down the back of his shirt. At least he hoped it was dirt. He stretched his arms outward in an attempt to gauge the dimensions of his foreboding tomb, starting with reaching out in front of him and then to each of his sides. Each time his fingertips hit the barrier before his arms were at full length, his elbows remaining bent.

Christian tilted his chin upward to look where the sky should have been but in its place was only more darkness. When he squinted his eyes and strained to see, he thought he could make out the outline of the weathered, splintery, hand cut pine boards of the door inches above his head. He could crouch but not sit. No matter how he twisted and turned, his knees would painfully strike the sides before his butt met the ground. The slickness of the onion skins littering the floor made keeping his feet in one place almost impossible. More than once, an attempt at adjusting his position ended with his knees meeting one wall or another with significant force while the back of his skull cracked against another.

Christian tried in vain to clear away the offending onion skins but no matter how he turned, stretched or tilted, he couldn't extend his fingers to the floor. The only thing that worked at all was pressing his back firmly against one side of his cell, balancing on his left leg and using his right foot like a broom, to push the debris in one direction and then the other. He was usually able to maintain his balance for two or three sweeps, but inevitably he found himself falling with his right shoulder and ear slamming hard into the unforgiving cement.

Like everything else in the barn, the cement was at least 75 years old, and had been poured long before the local home improvement stores started selling mixes that used extra fine gravel to make it smooth. This was a homemade concoction of gravel, small rocks, crushed stone, powdered clay, and limestone. It was sturdy and would probably last forever, like the pyramids. Unlike the new mixes, which are meant to be smooth as well as beautiful, this old version was all about functionality, and certainly not about the aesthetics at all.

Stones, gravel, and other sharp things stuck out at odd angles, cutting and scraping any of Christian's exposed skin that had the unfortunate opportunity to make contact with the jagged edges. After each fall, he peeled himself off the wall, leaving some skin and blood behind. The right side of his face throbbed and he could feel a dampness forming in his hair, his own blood causing it to stick together before the same blood dripped down into his ear.

A dozen or so attempts later, Christian had managed to clear a spot large enough for both of his feet to get traction. Now that his base was as stable as it was likely going to get, he turned his attention to the door above him. Christian reached up through the oppressive darkness and felt around along the underside of the door. Splinters poked and prodded his tiny fingers as they searched. On the far right side, he found what he was looking for-the hinges.

Three rusty metal hinges attached the door to a shorter row of planks that extended about eight inches out over the hole. He gave each a slight tug and found a small amount of looseness with the one nearest to him. The other two were much more snug and would be of no use. He repeated this process on the left side of the door, but found the sliding lock to be as tight as a snare drum. Bracing his feet, Christian placed one hand on each side of the single weakened hinge, squatted as low as he could comfortably get, and called upon every last bit of strength that remained in his body. His thighs and shoulders burned as he drove his feet straight downward and pushed up as hard as possible against the weak spot above his head. The semi-rotted wood flexed and a grinding squeak emanated from the oxidized metal, but the door would not give. Mr. Melanson must have rolled a bale of hay or two over the door.

"I'm sorry. Please let me out! I won't say anything, I promise. PLEASE!" Christian's begging voice came out sounding like a mixture of screaming and sobbing. His first words since getting locked in the tiny 3 foot long by 3 foot wide by 5 foot deep root cellar were 100% full of fear, betraying his usually brave demeanor. He was more terrified than he could ever remember being in the entirety of his nine years on earth.

Christian's pleas went unanswered; his squeaky voice echoing in the barn above, causing him to feel even more alone. His, now confirmed, solitude only multiplied the horror he felt inside. In his mind, he might as well have been the last person left in the world. Waves of nausea overtook him and he had to choke back the acrid bile as it came rushing up into his throat. His head swam and spun, made worse by being unable to see anything at all in the darkness. His heart pounded, sounding like war drums in his ears, ready to burst through his small chest at any second. Adrenaline surged from the terror, and he summoned every ounce of strength that he could find for one final attempt at pushing his way through the door and into the freedom of the cool night air.

Unfortunately, much like the last attempt, nothing happened—no perceivable movement all. With the adrenaline fully dissipated, he could feel his head starting to throb, his face flushing to the point where he expected his cheeks to start glowing. Beads of cold sweat developed on his forehead and rolled into his eyes, the saltiness adding to the burning that was already there, compounding his discomfort. All of his muscles were sore and shaking. With all prospects for escape dashed and fading into memory, he tried the only option he had left.

"Please! Please, let me out! I didn't see anything, I promise."

That last part was not the truth, but Christian hoped that Mr. Melanson would believe him, if he was even listening. He had actually seen "something" but he was not sure what that "something" was. All that Christian knew for sure was that he had snuck into the barn's upper loft to see why the light was still on when Mr. Melanson had supposedly gone to hang out with his buddies for the night.

After hearing some noises, Christian had crept along the floor, staying as low to the ground as he could until he reached the edge of the loft overlooking the rest of the barn. In the center of the hay-strewn floor was a very dirty man with a scruffy beard, tattered clothes that looked to be at least two sizes too large, and a look of sheer, unadulterated terror in his eyes. This unknown man had looked as scared as Christian felt at this very moment. The stranger was sitting in a chair with ropes around each wrist, his ankles, his stomach and another around his neck. He was just sitting there in the middle of the barn floor, but Christian didn't know why.

He heard a creaking behind him, followed by the darkness of a hand over his eyes. A second palm over his mouth and nose made it difficult to breathe. The hand blindfolding him moved to his chest, and he could see the loft disappearing behind him as he was dragged away from his perch. His feet banged against each step of the stairs. When they reached the ground level, he was tossed over Mr. Melanson's left shoulder, the familiar smell of cheap, hand rolled cigarettes, and even cheaper whiskey, made the new luxury of breathing again far less appealing. The last thing he saw was the open root cellar coming at him as he was tossed downward like a rag doll the door slamming shut above his head. Darkness closed in around him.

"I want to go to my room. I am sorry!", Christian yelled as loudly as he could while the small root cellar began to feel smaller and smaller.

Suddenly, out of nowhere, there was a loud scraping noise, the wooden door above his head creaked, and then light broke up the darkness. Not a lot of light, just a small amount seeping in through the spaces between the old pine boards of the door.

Peering through the tiny cracks, Christian could see a narrow section of the room above him. A small antique Coleman lantern sat on a picnic table about 15 or 20 feet away, and there were a couple more spread throughout the room. These were the lanterns that Mr. Melanson normally used to light up the barn when he was repairing his tractor or working on some other project. Christian couldn't make out a lot of what was happening; mainly he just saw shadows moving around. When a large shadow moved closer, he called out.

"Mr. Melanson, I have learned my lesson, can I please..." his words were cut off by any eerily calm but extremely angry voice.

"You need to be quiet now. You can come out when I am done. I would already be done if you hadn't interrupted me, and you know damn well that I hate to be interrupted."

Christian crouched in silence, surrounded by darkness. He was scared about what might happen – scared to move, but also afraid of staying where he was. He stuck his fingers out through one of the wider gaps on the left side of the door near the lock. The two fingers searched in frantic silence, hoping to find the small metal bar that slid into the metal loop on the other side. He found it!

The circular knob that normally sat on top of the slide bar was turned to the side and in the full lock position. Christian would need to push the knob back to the top position and then backward to be able to slide it out of the loop. He went through the motions in his mind and then tried to get his fingers to replicate those same motions. He wiggled the knob and managed to move it into position, but this minor victory came at a cost.

The old lock made a metallic grinding noise as it moved. Slowly, ever so slowly, he continued to move it towards the goal. Centimeter by centimeter, it crept along. The grinding noise seemed deafening in the silence, but he was almost there!

Suddenly, he saw a rapidly moving shadow rushing towards him. He simultaneously felt a searing pain and heard the crunch of bone against unforgiving metal and wood as Mr. Melanson's boot came crashing down onto his helplessly exposed fingers. Christian screamed in pain as he tried to pull his badly injured fingers back through the opening. The boot did not lift up; instead it twisted and crushed his fingers between the wood and the hard rubber sole.

Finally, the boot was gone and Christian had his hand back. He slumped down with his back against the cold cement once again, and his knees scraped against the opposing wall. Blood trickled down his shins but he barely noticed. He made himself as small as he could and clutched his possibly broken fingers with his only functioning hand. The sensation of a warm wetness filling his hand and something hard sticking out of the skin all but confirmed his diagnosis. It was possible that there was a huge splinter stuck into his finger but he doubted it. He was too scared to look, but he was pretty sure that it was one of his smashed finger bones.

"I told you I would let you out!" Mr. Melanson yelled down at him. "How am I supposed to trust you if you won't listen? You need to learn some respect, boy."

The hulking shadow standing over his makeshift tomb disappeared but Christian still didn't dare to move. He continued to sit in his crouching position and held his throbbing, likely broken, fingers in his good hand. He squatted there for what seemed like hours, but was probably only a few minutes, in complete silence.

The angry stomping of footsteps shattered the quietness, and the room became darker again. A chair was placed over the top of his door, blocking more than half of his available light. The ease with which the chair was moved indicated that it was empty, but it didn't stay that way for long.

The next sounds came from what appeared to be the tied-up stranger being forcibly dragged over to the chair. He was fighting as valiantly as he could, but being as restrained as he was, he didn't stand a chance. The door creaked from the weight of the man being slammed into a seated position on the chair. As Mr. Melanson tied the man down, Christian could hear the stranger crying and pleading through the tape that covered his mouth.

"Now I'm going to take the tape off but I do not want you to scream. Do you understand? No one can hear you out here and screaming will just make me upset. You DO NOT want to make me upset. Do you understand?" Melanson said in the same eerily calm voice.

A muffled sound of apparent agreement was followed by the tearing off of the tape. The man seemingly had agreed to stay quiet, but he didn't for long. Almost immediately, he began pleading his case.

"Mister, I have a family. Please let me go. I won't say nothing to no one. I swear. You won't ever see me again, I promise," the dirty, tied-up man sobbed.

"Did you hear that, Christian? He has a family. He says he won't tell anyone. Do you believe him?" Mr. Melanson asked, but Christian was still too scared to respond. "Sorry friend, this isn't your lucky day. It doesn't sound like Christian believes you either."

"Please, no, you can believe me. You have to," the man begged. Once again, his pleas became muffled; the tape was placed back over his mouth. He frantically started thrashing around in his chair and screaming, trying to get somebody's attention, anybody's. Sadly for him, there were only two other people in the room: one that couldn't help him, and the other was the source of his problems.

Christian heard Mr. Melanson walk away. It sounded as though he stopped at the far wall where he kept most of his farming tools. The man above Christian continued screaming and wiggling in a feeble attempt to escape, but he was not having any luck. Above the sound of screams, Christian could hear the scraping of metal tools against corkboard, and then footsteps as Mr. Melanson returned.

Something that the stranger saw must have frightened him, because he became more frantic. His attempts to escape became so vigorous that as he rocked from side to side, his chair began to tip. He was successful in getting the chair to tip over, and he crashed with it to the floor, nearly falling through the wooden door. He wiggled and wiggled but he was now stuck on the cellar door above Christian. Christian covered his head and flinched, but the door held. A new smell filled the small space of the root cellar. This man had gone a long time without bathing—

much longer than Mrs. Melanson would ever let Christian get away with.

Melanson's boots came to a stop just outside the edge of the door. The smelly man screamed and screamed. The boards separating him from Christian creaked mightily, and then came the creepiest sound that Christian had ever heard. It was laughter, but not the laughter of someone watching something funny, there was a demented sickness behind the laughter that made Christian's blood run cold. The more the man struggled, the louder Melanson laughed. After a moment or two, the laughter stopped, and Mr. Melanson spoke once again.

"I am sure that you would agree this has been fun, but I am expected elsewhere and Christian has already made me late."

The man struggled and screamed as Mr. Melanson struck him with whatever tool he had brought back from the corkboard. Each violent swing was accompanied by a sound similar to wet Styrofoam being stomped on. The blows continued to rain down. One became two, which became five, and then ten. Somewhere along the way the man stopped struggling, but the blows kept coming. Mr. Melanson repeatedly struck the man long after the gurgling sounds of his breathing stopped. Finally, mercifully, Christian heard Mr. Melanson walk away.

A new, sickeningly sweet smell took the place of the dirt, onions, and even the filthy man's body odor. Christian's face began to feel wet as something dripped on him from above. Feelings of nausea returned as he figured out where the wetness and smell were coming from.

Mr. Melanson returned and knelt over the presumably dead man. Through the small cracks in the door, Christian could see the outline of what Mr. Melanson was holding in his right hand, and a different kind of fear gripped him. In Mr. Melanson's hand was the antler-handled Damascus steel skinning knife that he took with him on deer hunts—some during the legal hunting season, some not. He normally used it to field dress and clean the deer, and the other animals that he slaughtered around the farm. Many pigs, chickens, turkeys, and even a few cows, had been skinned by that very knife.

He set the knife down on top of the door next to the unmoving man. He then reached over and grabbed the hook from his pulley that he used to hang up deer. He put the hook through the ropes that bound the man's feet, and then walked over to the far wall again. He pulled on the rope and the man slowly began to rise from the floor just as many deer, moose, and large game animals had in the past. He looped the rope around the hook on the wall and left the man hanging by his feet, the tips of his fingers lightly scraping against the door as he gently swung back and forth.

"Gotta get the blood out of him or the meat will turn bad," Mr. Melanson matter of a factly stated, as if what he was doing was no different than preparing a deer.

Christian watched in silent horror as Mr. Melanson knelt down, picked up his knife, and stepped toward the motionless man hanging by his feet from the rafters of the barn. He grabbed a tuft of the man's unruly, greasy hair and pulled his head back, exposing his neck. With a single, quick, seemingly practiced motion, the obsessively sharpened blade sliced deeply into the man's throat, nearly decapitating him. Only the bones of his spine kept his head from crashing to the floor.

For an instant, the man appeared to be alive, his eyes flew open, wild with fear. His return to consciousness was very brief and he soon went limp again. Blood poured out of his severed arteries and veins, showering down onto Christian like a thick, sticky, warm waterfall. The blood coated Christian's hair and descended down his body. His clothes stuck to him. Blood filled his shoes and his socks felt like warm sponges encapsulating his toes. When he tried to breathe, blood filled his mouth and nose with a metallic gelatin. The world began to spin, slowly at first and then faster and faster as everything became draped in a crimson hue, and then he fell into a black nothingness as the world faded away.

Cleansing Evil Description and Amazon links

From the outside, Dr. Christian Rinaldi has the perfect life. He is a good looking psychiatrist with a thriving practice, more than a dozen best-selling novels, a beautiful home and every toy that a man could possibly want. Sure, he also has a demanding boss, needy friends, recurring nightmares from childhood traumas, a nosy housemate, severe trust issues and a bad habit that he can't seem to shake, but who doesn't?

Christian's issues are slightly different than the average person's. His demanding boss is the head of a 700 year old secret society of serial killers. His friends? All but two are serial killers themselves. His nightmares are of his foster father who forced him to kill. Even his secrets have secrets. The biggest secret isn't even that he is a killer. His biggest secret is that he doesn't want to do it anymore. Unfortunately, his boss doesn't let his employees walk away.

Special Agent Randy Brooks, Christian's FBI liaison, doesn't know anything about Christian's secret life. He just needs Christian to help him solve their current case – a series of brutal but seemingly unrelated murders. Unfortunately for Christian, to get to the bottom of the crimes, he will have to confront his deepest fears.

http://www.amazon.com/dp/B00LK877ES

About the Author

Derek was raised in a small town in Down East Maine and after traveling for most of his early 20s, he returned to Maine to settle down and raise a family. He is now a married father of the three best children he could ever hope to have. He discovered his passion for story telling via writing in his early teens but didn't start writing professionally until nearly a decade later. He chose to become a ghost writer and write for other people rather than writing under his own name until last year. During his ghost writing period, he completed 6 novels and 100s of articles in various fields. In early 2014, with significant support from his wife, Janene, he took the plunge and released his first books under his own name.

Derek released "The Pilot Program" in May of 2014 as a nonfiction work aimed at helping others who suffer from panic attacks, anxiety or depression. Its publication coincided with National Mental Health Awareness Month. His second release was "Cleansing Evil", book one in a planned long running series revolving around a secret world of serial killers who wish to use their talents to cleanse the world by ridding it of its most evil inhabitants. "Cleansing Evil" was released on July 6, 2014 and by the end of its first day, had reached the Amazon Best Sellers list in 6 categories - ranking in the top 20 in most.

Due to many requests from his readers, Derek is currently writing a series of novellas to share the backstories of many of the minor characters inside the world of "Cleansing Evil". The first of which, "The Art of Death", was released on August 4. A prequel to Cleansing Evil is due for release in September. The second full length novel will be released in early fall with no less than 1 more planned by the holidays. Derek plans to release no less than 5 books a year. They will be a mixture of his current series and his many other projects which include everything from standalone horror works to a dystopian future trilogy to a romance series.

Derek can be reached on Facebook as Author Derek Dorr and on twitter as @DerekDorrAuthor.